Christmas Ghosties

Christmas Ghosties

Tales for a Winter Night

Rosemary Pavey

The Midnight Oil Artisan Press

2014

Published by The Midnight Oil Artisan Press 2014

Cover illustration and design by Rosemary Pavey

The Midnight Oil Artisan Press
www.paveypenandpaint.com

Printed by Createspace

ISBN: 978-0-9927463-2-2

Dedication and Preamble

To Lizie

and the magical bookshops of old Brighton...

The bookshops of old Brighton; an archipelago of dreams, with their dark corners and cramped stairways, their bargain basements, impossible, high shelves and wooden floors. Where else could one have found the leather-bound volumes, dog-eared, foxed and shaken, gilt-edged, broken-backed and inscribed in copper-plate, with which we began our fledgling libraries? What matter if they were written in Greek? They smelt of erudition.

Brighton's bookshop haunts were my first university, promising treasures beyond price for pocket-money pence. And now their memory is an archive of lost time. The stories printed here were written, one per year, as Christmas presents for family and friends. They are soaked in the shadows and mystery, the wet-winter-afternoon atmosphere of my formative book-hunts in the Lanes. To come home for tea and crumpets, with a haul of unknown titles to read by the fire, such luxury was all the sweeter for suffering the chills, the waiting at bus stops, the pavement-weary feet that a trip to town entailed...

What better nursery could there have been for a lifelong lover of words? And is it any wonder if I still catch myself listening for whispers and footsteps in the dark, and wondering what tales things have to tell?

Acknowledgement
My grateful thanks to all who have helped me in the creation of
this book and without whose patience and goodwill nothing
could have been accomplished.

The Author
Rosemary Pavey was born in 1960 and works as a writer and
painter in Sussex, dividing her time between her studio at the
Turner Dumbrell Workshops, Ditchling and Stoneywish, a local
Nature Reserve.

Also by Rosemary Pavey

**These titles are available from www.Amazon.com/co.uk or
direct from the author.**

The Beehive Cluster - *A Novel for all Ages*
The Magpie's Nest - *A Summer School*

Forthcoming Titles
Painting and Chaos
News from Stoneywish
A Cuckoo in Hell

To find out more about any of these or exhibitions, talks and
other events please visit: *www.paveypenandpaint.com*

Contents

The Last Parcel
A Christmas Fable

The Last Parcel
A Christmas Fable

Prologue
Or time to Settle Comfortably

It all began in Brighton.

Brighton has had so many incarnations, that at any chosen moment, in any given place, you may find several different towns there, jostling, cheek by jowl. Everyone knows of Regency Brighton and Theatrical Brighton and Naughty Brighton. These are commercial. But the process of re-invention goes on.

Amidst the clamour of any assertive here-and-now, lie hints of a future soon to oust all rivals, while the cast-off echoes of the past eke out their days in forgotten corners and alleys. Yesterday's centre of fashion has become a car park and architects are already competing to pitch new offices there. The lines which divide the town's chic from its shabby quarters are scarcely more permanent. A code of paint and potted plants may tell whether a street is going 'up' or 'down'. Yet the tide of social progress never rests and such boundaries move about from year to year. Slums which were once avoided by nice people casually become the new places to be seen in, while former hotspots languish. It is therefore not uncommon for a native of old Brighton to feel lost in the new city and for contemporary designer-shoppers to have scant knowledge of their own back streets. The nightclubs and retirement flats of the sea-front inhabit parallel but mutually exclusive worlds. Yet, however complete each present claims to be, clues to other, hidden worlds survive. And, versed in a topography of bracket-lamps and neglected dustbin-yards, the ghosts of the past still quietly fumble about.

Take the brass door-handle of this crêperie bar. Now cream and chrome, behind its Georgian façade, the business is fast and cheap and new. It belongs to a modern town. But the handle quietly tells

3

another tale. It is all that remains of Charnel's bookshop and it alone is enough to take you back thirty years to a vanished world when Brighton meant curios and books.

In those days there were so many second-hand bookshops, it could take an entire day to trawl them through and I can remember every step of the route that threaded the crowded Lanes; the atmosphere of each building; the characters of the owners, from the snooty man in 'Bequith's', to the lady near the theatre, who surprised us all one day by growing a beard. At the heart of this archipelago stood Charnel's, a seemingly imperishable place, whose proprietor lives on in my mind as a bald-headed bachelor with a stutter. For all his kindliness he was a man so nervous we wondered if he had had an overbearing mother or suffered some misfortune in the war. But Filbert, who outlived him by some years, once put me right on the matter. He didn't always have a stutter. In fact, he was quite a dandy and joker in his youth. Something strange happened to him one winter and he was never the same again.

Part I
Christmas Eve

Christmas Eve. Brighton, 1949. A steady, cold drizzle had set in and all morning Geoffrey Charnel had watched the pedestrians' umbrellas bump uneasily past one another in the street beyond his bookshop. After lunch the town had quietly emptied. It would be dark early today. From his window he enjoyed an unobstructed view of two roads: Ship Street, which passed the main Post Office and headed on down to the sea and Duke Street, running west, where the rival firm of Filbert and Wadlow had their business. He liked to keep an eye on them, though he had little competition to fear. Charnel's was the more ancient establishment, and boasted an exclusive, if smaller stock. As a novice, Geoffrey had learnt from his grandfather that books were only half the business, and that the

4

best booksellers were those who could read their customers. Now, comfortably established in his own right, he certainly knew *his*. They were Brightonians of the old school, then still-numerous: eccentrics with theatrical or literary connections; faded dears in mousy furs; ghosts of schoolmasters. Dear, old, dead dormice, he liked to call them - each clinging to a shred of distinction - a term at Oxford, a meeting with deceased nobility. They would be tucked up now in their cold little flats, crouched over the last of the gas before their metres ran out, and staunchly sipping the sherry or port that bound them to memories of sweeter days. Hey ho! Just now, he was young enough to feel detached from their mortality.

Not long till closing time. In a few minutes, he would slip along to the game-butcher's stall and collect his pheasant for tomorrow's dinner and soon he would be home. His sister Ethel was coming to cook and he had bought her soap - three pink bars in a floral box. As daylight faded and the temperature fell outside, the panes of the shop window rimed with mist; the interior seemed secret as a cave. For someone descending from the town it would have been hard, at first glance, to tell whether Charnel's was actually open. But this was nothing new. Situated at this junction of two roads, the narrow building belonged somehow to neither, but hugged a corner all its own. Gilt lettering, sign-written almost the length of the façade, announced, in the Victorian style: *'Antiquarian Booksellers - Musical Scores - Fine Bindings - Prints'*, yet for all that, it remained an unassuming place and easy to pass over. Inside, you stepped into another world. The air was suffused with the peppery smell of old paper. And the books... Books were *everywhere*. In low cabinets with glass fronts. In cages. In racks. And lining every inch of wall, where wooden step-ladders invited a perilous ascent to the ceiling. They sidled up the stairs to dusty upper floors and down to a crypt-like basement where the unwary tripped over uneven drains. From the humblest *'Everyman, I will be thy guide'* to red morocco with gold tooling, Charnel's crammed them in and the bookseller himself, sandy-haired, affable, talkative, unlike some snobs in the trade, had time to chaff with all.

Tonight, however, he felt unusually eager to be off. He had returned to his office to count the takings and warm his legs at the

5

electric fire, but no sooner had he opened the drawer which served as a till, than the door bell jangled and a pair of customers came in. Charnel gave an uncharacteristic start and closed the drawer, peering through the grill of the office window.

In the half-light he noted a short, elderly man in a shovel hat and a striking-looking woman, whose suit was fashionably tailored at the waist. Young, he guessed, though her upper face was hidden by a veil and her cheeks half-sunk into the fur of a fox tippet. A blast of freezing air blew in behind them.

"How can I help?" Geoffrey emerged, masking his irritation with a smile. Customers at closing-time were always a vexation. Today he felt on edge, unlike himself. Today, Christian as he was, he could have wished them to the devil.

"Ah!" The clergyman beamed as though he had already found what he was looking for. "Mr. Charnel! Florian's the name. Canon Wilfred Florian." He held out a papery hand. "And this - this young lady is my niece." Her eyes glittered behind their net. "We've come about the Codex - the manuscript from Granada." He spoke in a confidential tone, as if resuming a conversation only recently interrupted. "I take it you still have the document safe?"

Lethal as a dentist's probe, the question hit a nerve. As a rule, Geoffrey liked obscure requests - the more arcane the better. But today was different. Today he experienced an irrational sense of dread and the enquiry, so innocently delivered, sent his mind into a whirl. He blenched and took a backward step. His mouth went dry; his breathing stopped. Christmas was surely ruined now. He had been so looking forward to slipping quietly away. Taking a proper holiday. And he had so nearly *done* it. Why, oh why had he not locked up earlier? He was not made for adventures, disturbances. He liked the life he knew - ordinary and uneventful as the bus route home. He gazed in disbelief at the old man smiling there.

Today something queer had happened - something altogether uncomfortable and regrettable, which he had tried to dismiss from his thoughts. Yet, if the Canon had been a clairvoyant or a surgeon, he could not have pinpointed the spot with greater accuracy. The Moorish Codex; an ancient palimpsest; a bookseller's legend... Yes, unbelievably, it was here, though it had arrived only a few hours ago and amidst such mystery he could not for his life understand how knowledge of it had got out. He had been effectively saddled with the thing before he had time to reflect upon it and when he did reflect afterwards, his uneasiness grew and grew. Already he had the air of one inculpated in a crime. And the genial familiarity of this stranger now, filled him with little short of panic. *How* did he know about the Codex? The thing was impossible. Geoffrey had told no one. He had hardly seen a soul all afternoon. He had the horrible sensation that reality, his comfortable, customary reality, was sliding away, leaving him in the fear-infected landscape of a dream.

He returned a sickly smile: yes, he had it all right. Safe under lock and key.

The day had begun to go wrong after lunch, when a man wearing a black gabardine came blundering in, a cloth-wrapped bundle wedged beneath his arm. Broad, he was, flat-footed, with a beret jammed on his head and he spoke in a foreign accent, so thick, it amounted almost to an impediment, his spittle flying freely when he talked. He had pinned the astonished bookseller in a corner, spluttering in a furtive whisper about Zagreb and the War and the Rosicrucian Order. Charnel was used to his 'eccentrics' and prided himself on understanding and providing for them, but this character came too close and reeked of garlic. No matter that he was a self-proclaimed Professor and poet of some standing, his presence was overpowering and left an unsavoury atmosphere.

"Ze Codex," he tapped the package, which he proceeded to untie, "has been hhidden for hhundreds of yearss. It is of the utmosst - utmosst importance - but you see - I cannot keep it. I ddo not ddare!" His moon-face glimmered. "Ziss is too deep for me. Ziss is no less zan ze ssecret of Deass itself! Paracelssuss!" He laid a hand, swollen, like a ham, on Geoffrey's arm. "I cannot hold it! I do not assk money. I assk - find it a ssafe home. You," the Professor's fat forefinger tapped his nose and then prodded his captive. "You know your business! You can get it to ze prroper aussorities. Hhow important it is I need hhardly tell you. In ze wrong handss - my God! - imagine what could hhappen! And after - after, you rreap ze good reward. I come back and show you my

7

poemss - Yess! But do not delay. Hhe may follow me, even here."
With that, he turned on his heel and was gone, leaving Charnel to
investigate the gift.

Of course he had heard of the Moorish Codex. Who had not?
Like all the great alchemical treatises, it was the stuff of myth, and
scores of copies and fakes had been circulating Europe for over a
thousand years. Rumour had it that one rested in the Vatican, no
less. But the critical chapter of incantations concerning Death, this
was invariably missing. And the rest - a kedgeree of spells, and
gazetteer of Believers Relics, all written in algebra and a language
known only to the followers of Zoroaster - the rest was gibberish,
as everyone knew. Paracelsus, Leonardo, Master John Dee - they
had all had a crack at it. Now, here was Professor Czerny, with his
onions and his sonnets from Zagreb...

Charnel pulled back the cloth. One thing was true. He *did* know
his business. He knew his vellum and his oak-gall ink. And if this
curio had only a couple of centuries' worth of pedigree, well, he
knew at least one man who would pay good money for it... No
sooner had he entertained the thought than a shudder passed
through his frame. *'The proper authorities'* the Professor had said.
And who might they be? The British Library? The Bodleian? The
Archbishop of Canterbury?

Living out retirement here, in this very town, the customer he
had first called to mind was, without doubt, altogether 'improper',
but an expert in the field; perhaps, in a sinister way, the best.
Already it was too late to unthink the idea and he shivered, as if he
had, like Faust, called up the image of something unclean.
Nonetheless, business was business, and though this character was
neither a pleasant person, nor someone he liked to encourage -
well, he did visit the shop from time to time.

In his mind's eye, he pictured the pathetic, pantomime shadow
of Mortimer Grail. Seducer, necromancer and self-proclaimed
Anti-Christ, he had hogged the social headlines before the war.
Now, a mere puppet in fancy dress, he weathered disgrace in a
cheap, seaside boarding house, but he had retained a certain raffish
pride and his presence still exerted persuasive powers. There was
an aura, one could not say exactly of evil, but of corruption, say - a

8

taint of old pigeon-blood, lingering about him still. He would stage-manage an appearance in the 'mystery and occult' corner of the shop, and linger there a while. Then vanish without buying. But he had money - and something more - a nose for what he wanted. One had the feeling that he had not yet finished his career, but was waiting to pull one final stunt...

Charnel cast the vision aside. No. The Professor was right: '*The proper authorities*' - and it came to him in a flash. Of course, the proper authorities were the Police. The old Professor was a fence, disposing of ill-gotten goods. And he had allowed *himself* to become party to the scam. Damn! Damn! Why could he not see it at the time? Why could he not anticipate the bad publicity that might ensue? And why, of all times in the year, should this happen on Christmas Eve, just when he wanted to go home and relax?

He had cursed the Professor and his book, and, unable to decipher any of the hieroglyphs it contained, wrapped the Codex once more in its cloth and locked it in the office cupboard. After Christmas he would act. No need to jump at shadows... But the rest of the afternoon dragged painfully by. The thought of the old magician haunted him and time and again he caught himself looking up, half expecting to see him cross the threshold.

With each passing hour Geoffrey became more firmly convinced that Grail was the last person who should have Codex. His much publicised experiments with the forces of the universe had resulted in more than one human tragedy: a suicidal wife, an unhinged accomplice - who knew how many other victims? - and though he was now reviled and shunned by all, one could hardly forget that he had once been fêted by men of rank and loved by débutantes. What might the living cadaver of today not do, if he could unlock Death's secrets at last? The idea left him chill and glassy-eyed and it took Canon Florian some vigorous arm-shaking to bring him round.

"I say, my dear chap, are you all right?"

Charnel looked into the cleric's eyes with a dawning relief. There was kindness there behind the spectacles and proper human warmth, one might say, Christian cheer. Whatever should such a man want with a sorcerer's handbook?

9

"Oh, my research has always been deep," the Canon seemed to read his mind again. "I'm taking work with me - spending Christmas with a dear friend in the country - well, our train leaves quite soon. We have cases to carry and I am not strong, though Lucy here takes care of me. I wonder if you would send it on for me - by post? I'll catch up with it, or it with me, when I arrive."

Geoffrey surveyed luggage stacked by the door. The lights in the street, now brighter than his own shop lamp, threw jagged panes of yellow across the floor.

"But you haven't seen the manuscript," he objected.

"Professor Czerny's word is good enough for me,"

"You know the Professor?"

"We have corresponded for many years," he smiled, adding, by way of a tease: "How else should I know you have the Codex?"

Once again Charnel pictured the anxious figure from Zagreb and heard him lisp out: *"But act fasst. Hhe may follow me, even here."*

"If you are concerned about the price," resumed the Canon, "I am more than happy to leave that up to you."

He pulled a cheque book from his inside pocket, but the bookseller's mind was made up. Regardless of any irregularity, he was determined to be rid of the volume. Be done with it. For any price, or none. He remembered his Christmas pheasant and his sister and his brain began to clear.

"One hundred pounds?" ventured the old man. And hearing no objection he penned the sum and signed off with a flourish, his expensive Sheaffer nib caressing the page. "You are thinking this is a strange transaction for a clergyman," he handed over his payment with a twinkle of good humour.

"Perhaps."

"I do not hold with blinkered faith."

"Indeed."

"If the Devil is in this book, then I shall find a way of squaring with him, you may be sure!" He was fumbling once more through his pockets and papers. "Ah, now you need the address. Yes – send to me - Canon Wilfred Florian," He dictated slowly as Geoffrey wrote: "Care of White Lodge, Braston, Near Lichfield,

10

Warwickshire. I do hope it doesn't snow. My heart is bad and we shall have to change our train. Thank heavens I have Lucy! But we shall be tucked up by a fire before midnight! Oh, and one more thing..." Gloves, glasses case, handkerchief - out came the pen again and a used envelope. "If the Professor, or *anyone* enquires about me, give them this note. Thank you. You have been so helpful. Oh, and a Merry Christmas! God bless you!"

Standing blankly by the door, Charnel watched his customers depart. At the corner they stopped; he to catch his breath and she to ease her hands. The cases must have been heavy. They had a long, uphill walk to the station, and the air cut now like a knife. It seemed uncertain that they would make it, frankly. But the parcel now... He had just a few minutes left to catch the post - no difficulty there, for he was a master of string and brown paper and the Post Office was on his doorstep. Then lock up.

He put up the boards to the threepenny shelves outside – pocket editions and torn bindings – they were cold and slightly damp, but they would survive all right. Then made a tour of the shop, switching off the lights. He double checked the basement - Religion, Philosophy, Supernatural - and the dark corner by the drain - Greek and Latin - then shot up the stairs as fast as his legs would carry him.

Christmas! Yes Christmas. Already his spirits were lifting. He had a bottle of sherry, which dear old Mrs. Cartright had brought him. Now the pheasant, and the bus and he would put this whole, nasty business out of mind. He turned his key in the lock with an end-of-term relish, shook the door by its handle, turned up his coat collar and stepped smartly into the street.

"Evening Mr. Wadlow," he tipped his hat to the old boy, who was wrestling with the awning to his shop. Perhaps the rain had congealed on the freezing bars. He allowed himself an inward smile.

"Oh, ah, Geoffrey - and a Merry Christmas to you!"

"Going to be a cold one, I think."

Mr. Wadlow nodded, envying Charnel his gloves and scarf. "I'll be glad to be home tonight."

"Merry Christmas!"

11

Past the subdued windows of the Trafalgar Inn opposite. Past Winches, the clock repairer, and the leather shop, with its hand-made brogues - all now closed or closing as the last pedestrians hurried home. Up Cranbourne Street to that curious Farm Yard where the road ran smack into the blank backs of houses; all bins and drainpipes. It was a hundred years or more since any rooster strutted there. But here was Chapman, the game-butcher, hands hugged under armpits to keep himself warm, his rabbits and partridges all but frozen on their rails. He would wait on a little longer yet, for there were always some who left their shopping till last, and the staff were still turning out from the offices.

"Any chance of a pheasant, Mr. Chapman?"

"I got a nice one, good and ripe."

Ethel would pluck it and dress it. Charnel surveyed the stall, gaily decked out with greenery. By the light of the hurricane lamps, everything seemed oddly animated: the rabbits' eyes winked; the quail feathers twitched.

"And I got some lovely pigeon."

"No, no thank you. There are just the two of us."

"I'll put you one in anyway - seeing as it's Christmas." The butcher grinned like a conspirator. Poached was it? The pigeon would not tell, but it needed to go and by such means the customers were enjoined to secrecy."

"I'll take a little bit of holly if you can spare it," said Charnel, indulging in some seasonal levity.

"Have it and welcome. Two and six the lot. Ta!"

It was daylight robbery, but he didn't care. "A Merry Christmas!"

"Yeah, yeah," he was already looking for his next plump customer. "Venison! Lovely pheasants!"

Someone was roasting chestnuts on the road above. The smoke and the enticing aroma drifted down and for a moment Charnel was tempted to follow them and take a look at the lights and the festive window-fronts. Then he decided against it. Home now. God, but it was cold! Slippery too. The drizzle had set in a film of ice, quite treacherous on these slopes. Better to get to the bus - and tea, and the Home Service. How glad he was to have a short journey home - not like that poor Canon and his niece. If this rain *was* snow further north, he could almost believe that their parcel would overtake them. What a curious business it all was, to be sure. Singular from the start.

By the time he returned, Wadlow had put up his awning, locked the shop and gone. Charnel's thoughts were full of the evening ahead. His metalled heels rang out along the pavement. He could almost smell the gas in the scullery - yes - slippers - tea and a ginger biscuit. His footsteps tapped it out. *Cup of tea and ginger biscuit, cup of tea and ginger biscuit, cup of tea...* Then, something caught his eye.

By the telephone box, outside his own shop door, he spotted a figure, lit by the Post Office lamp. There was nothing in itself objectionable in the figure but his heart skipped a beat and with a spasm of anxiety he turned out of his way, into Middle Street. Wouldn't go past the shop after all. Take a detour down here, towards the sea. Suddenly he hated the urgent sound of his feet, but, God be thanked – he knew his town. Down here was the Hippodrome, rather grand, and here... Quick as a flash, he slipped into an alley no more than a yard in width. The maze of thoroughfares he had entered now, so bewildering to visitors, made up the Lanes, the celebrated web of passages that threaded the original fisherman's quarter. Here, since before the sea claimed half of them, had been the hemp-shares, the fabled inns, the crook-necked hidey-holes of publican's yarns. He was proud to know them like the back of his hand, proud to know their history too and many was the customer he entertained with tales of Martha Gunn and the renegade Prince.

Down here was a walled garden, worthy of Venice, and an ancient fig, whose boughs, now loaded with unripe fruit, clawed their way overhead. Only two lamps in this alley and there! You came out into Ship Street and the familiar sound of traffic. One dodge across the road and the alley continued eastward, narrower still. Twittens, they called them here, cat-creeps in nearby Lewes.

This one, with forbidding, high flint walls and an inn at its farther end, had been the setting for a Regency caper. Charnel was on home territory now and his nerve returned. This was the kind of story he loved to tell to summer visitors. A place for tricksters, smugglers doubtless and general ne'er-do-wells - none more devious than Bullock, a gambling swell, who famously challenged a sportsman to a race. Bullock, who, matching his name - a gross, fat animal of a man - could scarcely run up anything but bills! He laid a heavy wager on his winning too, though he could not hope to do it, but he insisted on two conditions. First, he must have a head start in the race. (A negligible matter, everyone thought.) And second, he must choose the spot where they would compete. At the last moment, he revealed Black Lion Lane to be his choice. And since, in that narrow place, it was impossible for any man, however fit, to pass him, he won his bet with ease.

Charnel, like all good storytellers, kept the twist till last. Indeed, he reflected, one would be hard-pressed to pass a man of normal stature here... His mind tripped on, like his heels, with a comforting clatter.

'*Cup of tea and... Not long now.*' He had been rather clever, taking this short-cut...

As he approached the end, his heart suddenly contracted. Beneath the last lantern - green gas in a metal bracket - stood the same tall figure he had endeavoured to avoid, swathed in an opera cloak.

"Mr. Charnel," said the spectre with an oily familiarity. "Did you think to give me the slip?"

Charnel looked over his shoulder, considering flight. But he no longer believed he could escape. First the Professor, then the Canon, now this... This creature might forestall him in any place. He steadied his nerve and stumbled on.

"Mr. Grail," he gave a mirthless smile.

"You *know* why I am here," insisted the other. "I was disappointed that you did not wait for me at the shop. Surely, you must have known that I would come?" He turned upon the bookseller a face that struck chill to the bone. Not that his features themselves were unsightly, or grotesque, though they seemed exaggerated, as though heightened with black pencil, but - perhaps it was simply that Geoffrey had never seen him quite so close, or perhaps, he had been ill - the flesh had the consistency of old

14

Caerphilly, yellowing, waxy, pitted with decay. A mummy or a petrified corpse would have had more bloom of life.

"Mr. Grail, it is Christmas - and my sister is coming," faltered the younger man.

"Christmas is a very special time, as you know, Mr. Charnel, for those of us interested in other worlds."

"Indeed." He was wriggling now, clutching his shopping; trying to sidle past.

But the old sorcerer placed his hand on the opposite wall and blocked the way entirely with his cloak.

"Death - death, Mr. Charnel - is very close at Christmas. The 'others' are very close at Christmas."

Of course Geoffrey knew it from his Dickens and his M.R. James.

"So you see why it is so important for us to return to the shop together, to fetch the Codex which the good Professor left with you... why it is so important for me - for my work - to have it tonight..." The curd-like crust of his face yawned in a smile.

"*Tonight*." He insisted.

Charnel felt death everywhere around him. In the fetid breath that offended his nose, in the long-jointed fingers that gripped the wall - the insidious voice - every manifestation of this madman. He could almost believe the tosh that Grail put out, that he was an emissary of the Devil.

"Impossible!" he choked. "It's gone."

"Gone?"

"I sold it. An hour ago. I've already put it in the post."

"Sold it?" Comprehension was slow. "Sold it? But how?"

"To a clergyman."

The eyes, like boiled-eggs, bulged. "Impossible. You jest now at your peril!"

"No jest - I have the proof." Dropping his purchases, he fumbled in his wallet.

"Here, see for yourself!" There were sundry papers and receipts but the cheque from Coutts, cream and crisp, was unmistakable. It unfolded to reveal an inexplicable blank.

Mortimer laughed.

Geoffrey Charnel raked through the wallet again. Somewhere here... It had to be somewhere here... Out came the envelope bearing the Canon's script:

"Forward to Main Sorting Office,

Paradise Street." It read. *"Follow me if you dare."*

But at this the Satanist flew into a rage. "No, NO!" he roared. *"He* could not know. *He* could not do this. You! You devious worm. You are trying to trick me. You cannot deny me this last chance to complete my work. I will know Death's secret. You cannot prevent it..."

"I posted it!" sobbed Charnel. *"There!* There's my Post Office receipt!"

Mortimer rounded on him fully: "You are not a bookseller," he was rambling now. "No, not a bookseller. You are one of *them.* An angel. Do you think I summoned the Professor from Zagreb for *this?"* He surveyed the trembling bachelor with a look of horror. "You are not a bookseller. No. You come, carrying holly which has pierced a bird. You, of all despicable, low creatures - you are my nemesis!"

"I was tricked. There *was* a cheque. He wrote it."

"Was he alone?"

"No, there was a woman with him. She carried the bags."

"But the Codex - you must have looked," now he was pleading. "You must have looked. What did it say? What can you remember?"

"It was gibberish - hieroglyphs and ciphers."

"Fool! You fool! You'll pay! You'll all pay." He ground his teeth, hissing something that was scarcely recognisable as human speech; then dropped his hand and, shrinking back, began to scale the wall.

How he did it Geoffrey Charnel could never say. He simply reached up, like a long-legged spider and silently slithered away.

"The Codex belongs to me," he warned, leering above the lamp. "It was written for me. I won't be cheated. I won't!" And he disappeared into the upper darkness leaving nothing but a wisp of fen-fog in his place.

Shaken, Charnel stooped to recover his things. How dreadful. How completely beastly and dreadful! Imagine it - Christmas Eve! A cat yowled and skittered past him up the alley. Suddenly, more than ever, he craved his homely things - Ethel's knitted tea-cosy, his antimacassars, his fire-tongs. Faltering, his heel-caps resumed their pace. It had been a mistake to come this way, but look! Here was Black Lion Street and in a few moments more, East Street and the bustle of Castle Square. Then the Steine, the dark elms lacquered with ice and trapping the lamps in webs of splintered light.

Buses waited at the terminus, shining quietly, their windows bleared with steam. The blessed reassurance of the familiar! No. 13A. *His* bus. He climbed aboard, glad to see his habitual seat was free. And in safety of his corner, he recovered some composure. Perhaps he had got the better of Fate, after all - and quite proper too. What right did Grail have, what business, to be poking into life's mysteries, with his great long nose. Overcome death? He even *smelt* of the grave! Charnel had shown him. Had outwitted him. And he felt suddenly relieved to have been swindled over the cheque. No money had changed hands. No one now could implicate him in the matter. And the manuscript was gone. Good riddance to it!

"Tickets!" The bus conductor came and stood expectantly at his side.

Geoffrey dug deep into his overcoat, noticing with distaste a dark stain upon the sleeve. Must have brushed against something in the passage. How unpleasant.

"I've a ret-et-eturn here somewhere. T-to Elm Grove. Thank you." His attempts to wrest a smile in return fell flat. It would be a long, cold shift for the conductor. And he was puzzled to hear himself stutter like a fool. But he had no time to reflect upon the fact. At that moment the bus gave a violent shudder and roared into life. Lights flickered and the great windscreen wipers started up. Everyday things! His breath came easier now.

He settled himself more comfortably, pocketed his ticket and, clearing the steam from the window, allowed himself a smile. He had had a narrow escape. A rather clever escape. Of course, holly

17

was a great protector from evil, hence its place at the heart of Christmas. Holly was the Celtic King of the Winter, the keeper of Life... Perhaps he'd done the right thing after all. Perhaps he'd have a new story to top old Bullock. Wait till he told Ethel!

As the fantastic domes of the Pavilion swung into view, the passengers, inspecting their shopping, or talking in quiet voices, hardly noticed the antics of the character at the back. Now he seemed to giggle to himself, then broke off and looked around in alarm, then he continued talking softly, struggling with his consonants, scrutinising his reflection in the window. *Paradise Street, now, was that a true address?*

He searched once more for Canon Florian's cheque, but this time his wallet was empty. All trace of the Codex was gone.

Part II
Christmas Night

In Birmingham that night, the starlings had gone early to roost; the deafening clouds of birds that descended on the Town Hall and St. Martin's at dusk had been lost to sight in a freezing fog which had reduced the traffic to a crawl. Footsteps came and went on the pavements without ever a body to put to them. The streetlamps flared. Christmas singers had gone home. Even the Salvation Army had turned to the pubs for a warmer welcome. And the great department shops had closed their doors.

In empty businesses up and down the city, behind frosted glass and at the end of dim stairwells, shadowy paper chains and cards hung on, their revellers, departed. But at the GPO office in Paradise Street there was hardly a moment's slacking and every window blazed. Now, more than ever, it was critical to achieve absolute efficiency. The nation depended on it and the Post Office would not rest until every last card and parcel was delivered. All the same, there would be a good atmosphere for this shift - joking and gossip in the breaks - everyone eager to be done. But the mail kept coming in. Those wretched last minute parcels. And business post, which stopped for nothing.

As the night wore on and the vans drove up and left, there was no time to imagine where all these packages would go, or what they might contain. A sorter's hand and eye moved faster than a camera shutter. With one flick of the wrist they had sent a love letter to Erdington, an invoice to Yardley, a little card with a black border to some unlucky soul at Aston. The life of the city and all its neighbourhoods passed through their fingers: Birds' eggs from Caldey, gingerbread and bed-socks, and expensive French perfume, all anonymous behind their string and manila paper. All so extraordinary and taken for granted. A testament to life, which was also full of surprises.

Eleven o'clock. Twelve o'clock. The Museum Clock chimed out the hours. There was a pause as the sorters listened and then wished one another a Happy Christmas - and the bells of St. Martins and St. Philip's began to ring the new day in.

Billy Furness, a big man with a sunken chest, nodded and turned back to his work, feeling cold and ill. Every winter, every fog, he found it harder to breathe.

"Look at this - some bright joker has put one here for Lichfield. What'd it come here for?"

"Too much Christmas sherry!" said the next in line, a Scot with a granite jaw.

"It's not going to make it to Lichfield now."

"Sling it over Billy, it'll do."

"It'll have the devil of a job."

"It'll do, I say. Not our problem, anyway."

"We'll be done in an hour, and I'm off to my sweet bed," chipped in another.

"Got something nice for Maisie, Bill?"

"I expect we have - I don't do that side of things."

"You make the most of her this Christmas, do you hear?" The curly-headed Scotsman cast him a look. "She'll want those good memories of you when she gets older."

Billy weighed the rogue parcel in his hand and tossed it lightly across.

19

Most like she would. He and the parcel had just about the same business here. Simply passing through.

Part III
Christmas Day

The morning dawned blue and white in Warwickshire, with frozen puddles and a dusting of snow that crunched like glass underfoot.

Silver-point churches, frost-rimed hedgerows, steaming cow-yards, smoking chimneys, everything you would expect of a country Christmas.

It was the very last round of the season. The Braston postman, Albert Cribb, blew into his hands and mounted his bicycle once more. Four more houses to go and he was done. Damned glad too. He hadn't much feeling for this place - had been here only a few weeks and the long rides between cottages made wearisome, cold, solitary work at this time of year. He hadn't much feeling for Christmas, either. Since his wife had run off to Canada with her baby son, he had little time for family festivals. All this love and goodwill simply galled his heart. Christmas trees, fairy lights, children in mittens, plum-pudding - the lot. What could he hope to feel, with a son who should have been his, six thousand miles away, and lodgings in a house which smelt of cabbage? People were very kind. That simply made matters worse. At every house he heard excited voices, smelt things cooking, met the beauty of the fields with a frozen eye.

The parcels he carried were crammed with goodwill - paper kisses. At every door, folk greeted him with smiles and blessings, for everyone loves a postman at Christmas. And he dispensed their happiness without sharing it, dreading and dodging the festive spirit wherever it showed itself. Leastways, that is how he had intended it. Last night in a fit of gloom, he had drunk more than he ought at the Crossed Keys and passed empty pleasantries with the

20

barmaid. He was slightly hung-over now and accepting a tot of something warming from the villagers he visited had left him a little unstable.

Four more houses, and no more thinking. He blew into his gloves again and felt the brief warmth radiate to his knuckles.

That's what would be in there, he thought. That long floppy package. Gloves, or a scarf from wool that had been knitted and unpicked a few times over. This year, a sweater - next year, a hot water bottle cover. His mother did that sort of thing. He had an identical parcel from her, waiting at his digs. And it was dreadful to feel so ungrateful.

Three cards for '*April Cottage*'. Thankfully, nobody in and the beastly little terrier that always tried to nip his ankles had to content itself with yapping behind the door.

Then the 'gloves' and a long, slim package for the Misses Wright at '*Codlins*' - and a treacherous, icy, north facing path to negotiate. Something bulky and squashy for Colonel Piers-Stanton. His wife, in her apron, standing anxiously on the step. "A merry Christmas!" She handed back an envelope - his Christmas box - and dashed indoors.

Now the last one. '*White Lodge*'. A darned heavy parcel that had weighed him down the whole way. By rights, this one should have been delivered by cart, it came straight from the station, but the carter had to see to his horse and all before he could get back for lunch and he had a large family. Albert had agreed to take it for him. A Bible, he shouldn't wonder, for a Canon Florian. Never seen him. Perhaps he was a guest.

'*White Lodge*' was a pretty house with gothic windows, and a large privet hedge enclosing lawns and a sun-dial on a stone pediment. A red-ribboned wreath hung on the door.

Cribb pulled up by the garden gate. Each house he had passed this morning had seemed more inviting than the last, glimpsed through windows, or a crack in the door, with neat polished furniture, a cat in a porch, a half-folded newspaper, boots, wet with snow - everyone's lives so perfectly self-contained, now the war was over. He parked his bicycle, adjusted his hat. He himself had refused all invitations, hurt heaven knew how many friends, his own sister, his mother and their cushions and their coal scuttles - and now he had nothing to go back to but his own ill-temper and the smell of cabbage on the stairs.

He lifted the dolphin knocker, catching a squint of hallway with a study beyond. A homely woman in a cardigan opened the door.

"Morning. Parcel for the Canon," said Cribb, just touching his cap.

"Canon Florian?" she did not take the package.

"That's right. '*White Lodge*'."

"But, my dear, the Canon is not here. You're new, aren't you, so you would not know. The dear Canon died a couple of years ago."

She let the door swing wide.

"Are you family?" asked Cribb.

"Dear me, no, though I knew him of course. But how very strange and sad. And what do we do now?" Her eye took in the young man on the doorstep, sallow and underfed. "And you've gone to all the trouble of coming this far, and on Christmas morning too. You must be fairly frozen. Step in a moment and warm yourself. I'll call my husband. Bernard! Bernard! Do come down, my love. Such an odd thing!"

The hall was snug. A mongrel bitch padded out of the kitchen and nosed the postman's hand, her tail laconically wagging to and fro.

"It's all right" he said. "I can take it back again. There's a sender's address, look. Some bookshop in Brighton. They'll return it from the depot."

"But how curious." She affected not to hear. "Well, you know, he *was* a keen scholar. Some people here would have nothing to do with him because of his past - but *I* think he was an inspiration - a positive fountain of goodness and love - and the rest was just tittle-tattle."

"His past?"

"Now," she laid a motherly hand on his sleeve. "Have you time for a mince pie and a little sip of something to keep you going? I'm sure you have a family waiting eagerly at home. I don't want to delay you, but I've made rather a lot this year."

"I'm not in any hurry," said Albert, patting the dog on the head. "What past?"

"Oh, people will say all sorts. I expect you've heard a lot of it already. But I maintain the Canon was a deeply Christian man. He lived by example when he was at Lichfield and when he retired here, he did whatever he could for others, despite atrocious health."

"I haven't heard what they say."

With irritating propriety, she smiled: "Then it's not for me to tell you - certainly not at Christmas-time. Here - these are the hot ones. Take two! And a little sherry? Or perhaps you prefer something stronger. Bernard!" She turned to the stairs. "Come and meet this nice young man!"

"I suppose he'd got no family," said Albert, taking off his gloves and laying the parcel on one side. Suddenly, he had no wish to go out again. His feet ached unbearably as they began to thaw and his chilblains smarted.

"He had a *niece*..." Mrs Langton paused with the whisky bottle. "...who stayed with him at the end. A strange, cold woman. I didn't like her. Though she was here again visiting just the other week - well, just before you took over the round - yes - the very night poor Jack Hardman had his accident. Do you know the Hardman's yet? They're the last cottage down this lane before the big dairy farm on the Tamworth Road."

Cribb shook his head and slipped a morsel of pastry to the dog.

"Oh, the most terrible thing. They'd only been together again a couple of years, after coming through the separation of the war. He was out East, you know - had a bad time - and those two children such a handful - and the new baby just born. And no money. Well, you know what agricultural wages are. A fit young man like that! He slipped and fell under the horse when they were carting mangels. Well we've never seen mud like it - and that was a beast of a horse. Jeremy told me - He'd seen him play up no end of times."

"Did it kill him?"

"Oh yes- stone dead. Poor, dear girl. I feel so worried about her. I made up some things to take them, just a cake and some clothes for the children, but my knees started up again this morning and with all this ice about, I simply daren't trust myself in the lane."

She chirruped on and the whisky slipped comfortably down.

"I'm going that way," fibbed Albert, suddenly curious. "And I've got my bike. Give your things to me and I'll take them down there for you. It's my quickest way back to the office."

"There now! Do you see what I mean?" Mrs Langton beamed at him. "That's the dear Canon's goodness still at work. If his blessed parcel hadn't come, well, you wouldn't have knocked at the door, and I shouldn't have told you about Alice - and... You're a dear, good soul and you deserve a merry Christmas! Bernard! Come down and say goodbye. I didn't catch your name, my dear. I do hope you'll like it here!"

When the door closed behind him, Albert's ears were ringing. He placed the Canon's parcel and the charity bundle in his bicycle basket. *Last cottage before the farm*, she said. *Can't miss it.* It had touched him, this tale of another's misfortune and he felt a little ashamed of his own self-pitying. Perhaps the alcohol had made him sentimental, but he knew how it felt to lose everything at a stroke. And at a time like this...

Cycling slowly, so as not to jolt the cake, he slid from one frozen rut to another. The whisky sang in his head. He was no longer a loner, stranded in an alien landscape, but a man with a purpose - a man who was needed. His wheels hardly touched the ground. When a large motor-car approached, he gripped his handlebars, staring straight ahead. *Don't look down. Don't think. Don't blink or look at the driver.* He was tipsy, he realized. Christmas spirit! He braked at the bend and dismounted carefully. Better leave the bicycle here. Carry the parcels in his arms.

There was a flat stone bridge across a stream, then a path to the cottage, through an unkempt garden. But the path was moving, sliding about where the ice and water curdled together and his feet felt estranged from his body...

"Mom!" called Freddie, peering from the landing window. "Mom! Postman's just fallen in the ditch."

It took her a minute to hurry out and help. He was not hurt - not even seriously wet. He had landed upright in the stream, with his

24

packages gripped aloft - and the icy water felt quite pleasant to his senses, dizzy with sherry and hunger and the keen winter's air. But the sides of the ditch were steep and in his present confusion he stood stupefied, uncertain what to do.

"Lord have mercy. Are you all right?"

"Oh yes," he struggled to hold on to whole sentences. "I was bringing some things from the house up there - '*White Lodge*' - she sent you these for Christmas."

"Look at the state of you!"

Two ragamuffins, aged perhaps four and six, stared rudely from the bank. The mother, a girl in a wrap-across apron with tired eyes, hair in clips, was biting back the urge to laugh.

"And this package here's to go back." Albert handed over the parcels, adding sheepishly: "Look a right, silly fool, don't I?"

The children were sniggering now. "Get along in - you two," snapped Alice. "You'll catch your deaths!" Then, as he scrambled out, she gave a shrug. "I didn't mean to laugh. But you're right. You do. You haven't hurt yourself? Come up to the house and I'll find you some socks. We're not very tidy, mind. You'll have to make allowances."

She had a dry, capable way, as if she were used to calamities. Albert teetered behind her, planting his feet where she trod.

After the other houses in the village, this one came as a shock. It was sparse and comfortless. A muddle of washing and cooking filled the kitchen; the back door swung on its hinges.

"I was fetching the coal. We're all behind today."

"Please don't fret," said Albert. "I won't come in. I'll spoil the floor." The lino was covered in mud.

"You'll die of pneumonia, more like. The range is on, look. Put your things there and come through."

He wanted somehow to let her know that he understood, that he knew about her troubles, but he could not find the words and she ignored his sputterings. "You're our Father Christmas, aren't you? Don't mind the baby. Come on in and behave. We're not as bad as we look." She was pulling the clips out of her hair - scooping up the airing. "We'll be straight by lunch-time." She gave a smirk and he returned it. They were playing a game, he thought. Hold on tight and don't look round and everything will be just as we pretend.

"Mrs. Langton…" he began.

"She's a saint!" Alice cut him short. But her voice had the tone of a critic. "A real saint. Sit yourself there, look." She was unwrapping her goodwill gifts. "That's genuine Christian love, you see? Cake. And charity clothes. And chocolate." A queer look crossed her face. "How I hate it when people are kind! Look, *real* chocolate. The children won't believe their luck!"

She fled upstairs and Albert unlaced his boots. His feet were burning now and the sensation served to bring him round. He got up to close the door and brought in the bucket of coal. By the time she returned he was back at his chair.

"Has she been there long, Mrs. Langton?" The question was innocent enough.

"Only since the old Canon died."

"And he …"

"He was a saint too! They *all* are round here." This time she managed a grin. "Here, put these on - and I'll dry yours. You can collect them when you next come by. You're not superstitious are you? They were my husband's, but he's dead. And they're good socks. Too good to waste." There! It was out.

"Don't say it!" she continued. "I know. It can't be helped. The world is full of awful things but we just soldier on – all right?" She looked him square in the eye. "Won't you have a drink to warm you up?" Now a glint of mischief. "A cup of *tea*, perhaps?"

"A cup of tea would be grand." He thought he could sit happily here in this draughty hovel and never go back to the world that he had come from. The children had vanished, and he took in his surroundings with a passive eye. There were paper decorations, but no tree. The range was covered in ash. A dozen jobs had been begun and not completed, though someone had haphazardly laid the table. A shotgun hung in the corner...

"Why do you ask about the Canon?"

"That last package was for him. The woman at '*White Lodge*' mentioned something about his past."

"Oh, that." She was filling the kettle. "It is whispered that he did something wicked in his youth."

"Wicked?"

"Devil-worship!" she mouthed, teapot in one hand, strainer in the other. But then she was serious again. "He was caught up with a bad set - easy enough to do, God knows! Got away from them though - tried to atone for it all the rest of his life. Of course, for some people that's not enough. The stigma always stuck. But he was the genuine thing. Clever too, for all he looked so simple."

She turned round and dropped her defence.

"Look, I know I sound pretty hard and beastly, but I do know decent people when I see them. That Mrs. Langton has a heart of gold. And I'm not ungrateful. But the Canon never pretended to be perfect. He had a past. And it made him more human-like, able to understand. They said that he always had one ear cocked for danger. He was never forgiven for leaving that 'Brotherhood of Cain' and he was afraid that his old 'master' would come after him."

"How did he die?"

"In his bed, sleeping peacefully."

"And his niece?"

"That woman! I never could stick the sight of her, though he seemed happy enough with her at the end. She was creeping round here only a few weeks ago. They'd never got on and then suddenly he made his peace with her. Sugar?"

* * * * *

Freddie and Frances wandered outside again. Lunch would be late and it was better to keep moving, keep playing, than wait about for it. The dog, a muddy Airedale, joined them.

On the chair in the porch lay the postman's parcel and Freddie approached it, touched it, caressed it. It was a real Christmas present. Not just a sock with an orange in it - a real proper present. The postman was sitting in the kitchen, drinking tea. He'd brought the parcel for *them*. Freddie heard him say so. This was his last call. And his Mom was too busy to come and see to it. Freddie

27

couldn't remember seeing such a large present before, with so many stamps and important-looking labels.

The string was tightly knotted, but his tiny fingers could probe between the strands, lifting the edges and prizing the layers apart.

"What is it?" lisped Frances.

"It's something very important," he replied. "We should take it to the barn."

The barn was an outhouse where they stored the coal. Barley slept here when she was too dirty to come indoors. All serious schemes and games were planned in here. This was where they hid when they were wanted for 'chores'. Now they sat, oblivious to the cold, with the parcel between them, picking at the paper. Tentative at first, they gradually grew bolder, till, as the contents came to light, they tore at the thing with wild determination. They couldn't undo the knots, but Freddie had charge of his late father's knife and they cut the string.

"It's a book," said Frances, disappointed.

"Not just a book." Freddie was not going to give up on the moment now. "It's magic." He turned it over with a knowing air. "It's the most magic book in the world."

As a matter of fact, it *did* look different - different from the books his mother read him.

The pages, stiff and patterned with squiggly marks, would, he saw with deepening wonder, provide material for innumerable schemes: for boats, arrows, lanterns, coffins for burying things in, fans, propellers, fuses... Barley liked the smell of it. They could paint on it...

"Read it!" demanded Frances, her fat curls and pursed lips coming close.

"It says..." Freddie had never had any success with reading. Now he improvised, tracing the script with his finger. "*Abracadabra*! It's secret. It's a *really big* secret. And no one must ever know we've got it. It's *ours*, from Father Christmas. Understand?"

* * * * *

"Blimey, I must go," Albert jumped to his feet.

Alice set the baby down and wiped her hands on her apron. "Bring the socks back when you're passing."

"I will."

"And ride carefully!"

"Thanks, I will."

"And…" She rubbed her nose with the back of her finger. "Thanks for falling in the stream! You've cheered me up!"

Albert gave her a wink. "You have a Happy Christmas, now!" He meant it. He returned to his bike, crossing the bridge with exaggerated care, and wobbled away, his cap set at an angle. He was sorry not to have seen the kids. Trouble they were. She had said so. Always in trouble - running off - taking things. He himself had been just such a boy… He'd like to have given them something to play with.

He was so preoccupied with his thoughts and the sharp curve of Alice's hip, that he was half-way back to the depot before he remembered the Canon's parcel. Damn - oh damn! To lose a parcel would as good as lose him his job, but he couldn't go back now. Perhaps he could collect it tomorrow. Perhaps the Post Office would not notice the delay. Perhaps it was not such an important parcel and the sender would not enquire after it right away. It could hardly, after all, be a matter of Life and Death.

A week later the ice had turned to slush. The Moorish Codex was no more than a flotilla of little boats in the former dairyman's ditch and the postman at Braston made his round in his smart, woollen gloves, like a man with a new lease of life.

"Did you hear the news?" asked Alice at the gate.

"Did the packet turn up?" he half-hoped now that it wouldn't.

"No, but something peculiar happened".

She had done her hair early today and looked brighter, more animated.

"You were asking about the Canon. Well that man who nearly destroyed him years ago, the one who tried to sell him to the Devil - he's died at last. He was found on a rooftop in Brighton over Christmas. Frozen stiff he was. It was front page in the '*Echo*'." She paused. "Here! That parcel was from Brighton, wasn't it? Do

29

you think it was him that sent it? Well, neither of them will be wanting it now, will they?"

She was hoping he would not spot the litter at his feet.

Albert let her have her say. He had some toffee in his pocket for the children.

She went on thoughtfully, one foot swinging the gate.

"He spent the whole of his life trying to gain dominion over Death - that's what they said." Then she dismissed the matter with a snort: "Only silly fool, he forgot something very simple." She waited till he looked up and met her eyes.

"Love had already done it."

The Landmark

The Landmark

The Lamb Inn at Brackenthwaite was the latest casualty in the craze to modernize the old pubs of England. Times and customs were changing fast and the march towards all things clean and clutterless had swept away all the insanitary insignia of the past.

Gone were the hunting scenes, the rosy lampshades with their incomplete fringes and brown scorch-marks. Gone were the ashtrays, the frayed brocade, the horse-brasses and the toby jugs. Dark corners and yellowed ceilings, paper beer-mats with multiple ring-patterns, faded photographs of cricketers, gin-traps - all had been consigned to the displaced memories of the elderly, and in their place spread a ubiquitous wash of seawater greeny-grey, mortuary-clean walls, heavy gilt-framed mirrors, slabs of bare wood tables with fat altar-candles burning on them and a chains of fairy-lights at the bar. Paul Dombey's christening feast would have looked well there. The ingle-nook remained but a miserly fire of two logs was all that sputtered in it, and they appeared to be for decoration only. Other heat was hard to detect, and on such a filthy night as this, the draughts which found their way through gaps in the walls circulated freely, for the internal lath and plaster had been stripped away and the beams of the old 'snugs' stood naked as church pillars. The beer, now continental, came in glasses with stems. But customers were *expected* to order wine - wine from selected vineyards.

As for the menu, it flaunted dishes in exotic combinations: traditional steak and kidney with basil and kiwi jus, or sausage on beetroot mash; noisette of local venison, enisled with yam and rocket in a decorative puddle of something sweet and red. Strictly, no sandwiches.

The clientele had changed too. Old Matty Dixon, who had propped up the bar on his high stool for the last forty years, had been told that his side-chat disturbed the customers, and had taken to drinking alone at home. In his place, well-heeled tourists and the owners of holiday cottages exchanged the time of day. Walkers took their muddy boots to 'Jaspar's', a wine bar up the road. But the retired crew of the Brackenthwaite retained fire station clung on and for their Christmas reunion they had taken over the corner where the bell of their old engine still hung as a reminder of days when fire crews drank heartily before taking to the road, and landlords had need of a bell for calling 'time'.

There were six of them this year: the twins Jack and Thomas Barker, Noddy Perkins, Alf Skeps the sheep farmer, Will Kirby, who had retired early through ill-health and Joe Laughton who could still shin up a ladder and wield a chain-saw. They had lost a comrade to pneumonia earlier in the year, and a combination of threats from wives about mixing heart pills and alcohol had put them on half-rations at the bar, but their own spirits were undaunted. They seemed not to notice the corpse-flesh walls or the rain lashing down outside. They cheeked the bar-maid as though they were lads again. Their guffaws cut through the ambience of cool jazz and white musk room fragrance. They were in another place and time - a warmer, rosier, more genial place where the girls all loved them and the thrill of answering a fire call was such that in thirty years they had not once failed to turn out. The bond of brotherhood and old pride put a gloss on every memory - and this was the time for memories!

"Here, my darling," called Noddy, waving his glass at the counter. "Another one of these all round."

"Not me," Jack Barker put up the palm of his hand. "I've had enough, old lad."

"Enough? What kind of talk is that? We haven't even started yet and he's had enough. Tell him to pull himself together. This is your station officer telling you. Sit up straight and do as you're told." Noddy was only half in jest.

"'E never did as he was told," observed the sallow-faced Will.

"That's right enough! Do you bide the time we were putting the chains on the old fire engine, the winter of '67, and you asked him to roll it forward a bit - and he put it in reverse and crashed straight into the station wall?"

"Bloody nearly killed me too," beamed Noddy.

"And the day he had that whisky at MacIntyre's and you said turn right up Miller's Bank and he turned left and drove into the duck pond?"

An appreciative roar went up. "He was a damned good fireman, for all that. And I'll tell you something." A pause. "They don't make 'em like that today."

"That's the truth. Brackenthwaite have a struggle to muster a crew these days. They've not the dedication we had. They're off visiting somewhere, or having their dinner when the bleeper goes and they don't bother to turn out if they don't feel like it."

"It doesn't make much odds if they do," Thomas Barker added. "They can't do owt, not even climb a ladder unless a senior officer says so."

"It's small wonder they're demoralized."

"Look at that barn fire at Fell Farm. By the time the health and safety people had sorted themselves out the bloody thing had burnt to nothing."

"Old Sid was the one for barn fires," reflected Alf, remembering how the old-timer had once saved his own hay.

"Ah, poor old Sid. He was a daft bugger, but when it came to fires..."

Noddy winked as the barmaid returned with his drink. "Here's to old Sid. May he rest in peace."

"Do you remember when he got those cakes out of Brackenthwaite Bakery? They'd just loaded up the ovens when the building went up and he found them half-cooked in the ashes. Ate most of them too. He was sick as a dog!"

"And when he fell off the roof at The Landmark?"

"The big chimney fire!"

"He was going up a ladder with the hose-reel - no mucking about with cherry-pickers then - and he saw a girl in one of the bedrooms and was so overcome, he lost his footing and fell right off."

They were laughing now till the tears came. "Got concussion and swore after he'd seen a ghost!"

"That weren't what you think though," said Will quietly. He alone had kept his composure throughout the evening. *He* was the one they had expected to die and his yellow, hatchet face testified to the strain of long illness. He had been a chain-smoker and though he had been forced to quit, he still found it hard to swallow a drink without a fag. But he had always been a man apart, a sardonic onlooker to the fights and pranks of the others.

It was unusual for him to speak at all and a hush fell as he wiped his mouth with his hand and glanced around.

"When he was ill at the end, like, I went to see him and we got talking." The surprise and attention intensified. "He told me what really happened at the Landmark. And it wasn't nowt to do with a naked woman."

All knew The Landmark well. It was a coaching inn up on the moors at the highest point known as Gamma Peggy's Pass. The motorway had cut a new route to the west and Gamma Peggy's was now a road for tourists and locals only, but years ago it had been the main highroad of the region. On a night like this, the Landmark was the only hope of refuge for miles. Built like a fortress and famous for its hospitality, it was a welcome sight to travellers. It was also the devil to reach. On the evening of the famous chimney fire the Brackenthwaite crew had battled through snow to reach the spot. They could see the sparks flying from the bottom of the Steep but the wind was already whipping up drifts on the hills and it had taken their combined skills just to keep the machine on the road. Once there, they knew exactly how to proceed. One man on the pump, one man inside, one on the roof, directing the water down the chimney, one holding the ladder steady. This time there was ice to contend with as well and the radio man would fairly freeze at his post.

On a night like this... It had been raining now for a fortnight without a break and the moors were saturated like a giant sponge. The river at Brackenthwaite Cross ran, a black torrent, prickling with flecks of foam. Several walls were down where tributary streams had spilled over and taken short-cuts down the sides of the road. It would require some courage to step out into the weather tonight!

Will waited till they had had time to remember. "Sid was the second man to go up," he began. "I think you went first, Tom."

"Aye, that's right."

"You got the roof ladder hooked on the ridge - and he was coming up behind taking some of the weight of the hose-reel. Well in that old place there's a row of like servant's bedrooms with dormer windows in the roof and the windows open onto a narrow parapet. Sid gets half way up and suddenly he sees a child, standing on the ledge - a little girl - perhaps six or seven years old. Golden hair. Long nightie. It's snowing hard and there's a twenty-five foot drop to the ground. He calls up, but neither Tom nor the child can hear him, so he does what we all used to do in them days, he makes his own decision, goes on up, hitches his hose-reel over the end of the ladder and climbs onto the parapet himself. The child is cold as ice. He carries her back to the open window where her little candle is burning and sets her down inside.

"You stay there, my darling," he says. "You'll catch your death." But she won't go back to bed. She stays at the window and as he climbs back on the ladder, she flings out her arms and points to the open moor. "Look! Look!" she shrieks "The Landmark!" He turns and for a moment sees a light flaring far out across the snow. Then he loses his balance and - the rest you know."

"Damn near squashes Alf at the bottom!"

"He landed in a snow-drift, which saved his life. But he was unconscious for a time. And while we were toiling on outside, he was nursed and looked after in the warm, by the landlord's mother and his very pretty wife! He just about came round for the clearing up. We used to pride ourselves, as you'll recall, on leaving a place all clean and tidy, not like they do now, splashing water all over. And you have to be so careful with them old buildings in case the fire gets into one of the beams and smoulders and breaks out later on. Sid was still shook up and all he could say was that he'd seen a girl. There were lots of guests at the place that night and naturally we thought the obvious. Well you do see some funny things when you're on a fire call. Naked women wouldn't be the half of it."

There was a murmur of assent.

"Anyhow, Sid wanted to get back to that room so he offered to go up in the attic and check the rafters. The old lady went along to show him the way. There are doors from all those top bedrooms,

37

connecting with the attic landing and he thought he might get a chance to reassure himself like, that child was still okay. But the first door led straight into the roof-space and there, amidst a pile of junk, the first thing Sid sees is an old rocking horse and a heap of wooden toys. 'Those –' says the old lady, confidential like. 'Don't you go touching them. They're *her* toys.' *'Her toys?'* says he. 'The little girl that Gamma Peggy took in - back in 1824.' 'Tell me about that,' he asks, real earnest, like and seeing the queer look on his face, she doesn't like to refuse.

"'There was terrible snow that winter,' she begins, 'and one night the stage coach came off the road - further up on the moor. Nobody realized at first. The coachman must have missed the light of the Landmark up ahead and lost his way. It took six men, finally, to dig them out of the drift, but the appalling thing was that when they got to them, they found all the passengers dead - throats cut – all, but the little girl. Someone had robbed the mail. They brought the child here half-starved with cold and they advertised for her relatives in all the local towns. But no one came forward to claim her and do you know, they could never get her to say where she'd come from or what had happened that fateful night.

"'Peggy was the landlord's wife and she had no child of her own. She took to that little thing and loved her as if she had mothered her from the first. But it caused a deal of trouble here. Peggy's husband could not bear the sight of her sweet face and golden hair. Said she fair gave him the creeps. Lots of things gave him the creeps. The Sergeant at Arms for one and any mention of the Stage Coach disaster and though no one was ever convicted of the crime, Peggy and her husband were heard arguing about it over and over again and one day they found him in his own back stables. He'd hanged himself from a beam and the locals said he'd as good as admitted some guilt in the matter and passed sentence on himself. The Landmark was a lonely, rough, old place in those days and there were plenty of bad rumours about the goings-on here but after the suicide, things began to change.

"'Peggy took over the running of the inn and she adopted the little girl, proper like; sewed her clothes and bought her toys and coddled and fussed her like a princess. And it wasn't just the child she took care of. Travellers, who used to fear the pass, began to look forward to stopping by. The Inn got itself a reputation for a warm welcome and Christian cheer and the landlady of the Landmark became the legendary 'grandmother' of all. The child, though, never settled. Night after night, she would sit at her window, gazing out over the moors, and holding up her candle, in all weathers, looking for her murdered parents, local folk said. Others told a darker tale. It was sometimes said that the stage coach accident was no accident after all; that the coachman had been deliberately lured off the road by a false light and pulling up as he thought at the inn, he had tumbled straight into Dyer's Cut and the ambush that ended his life.' The old woman wanted to finish there but Sid was waiting for more.

"'The little girl?'

"'She died. Caught pneumonia no doubt, sitting up o' nights.' Nobody talked of the matter now. It was considered unlucky. Did he reckon the beams were safe? Well then, he needed to get home and rest himself. He'd had a nasty 'do' and he'd feel it in the morning."

There followed an uneasy pause. Then Alf shuffled his feet and coughed. "Told you that, did he? Well he told me it was a blonde. And a very nice one too!"

His irreverence brought them back to terra firma and the Brackenthwaite old retainers began to stretch and feel in their pockets, wondering who would be first to break the party up. But at that moment the manager took it upon himself to do the job. Muttering an apology he pushed amongst them and grabbing the rope of the old fire bell, called everyone to attention.

"Ladies and gentlemen, I'm sorry to interrupt your evening, especially seeing as it's so close to Christmas, but we've just heard some rather important news. The river has burst its banks downstream and part of the old bridge at Tollergate has been washed away. We strongly recommend that you go and get yourselves home right away, avoiding the Tollergate road. Any problems, please come and talk to us. The police are making alternative arrangements for people who are stranded."

That put an end to any festivities. The bar emptied as if by magic and Alf Skeps found himself out in the street in a blur of hail. The others could get home easily enough. They lived within spitting distance of the fire station still. But Alf had some way to go. As they made their hurried goodbyes, they heard the two-tone of the Brackenthwaite engine speeding out of town. It would be the youngsters' turn to prove their mettle tonight. Alf's farm lay just a mile or two away on the fell. His sheep were safely penned. His son would see to them, in any case. The Christmas lights rocked dementedly across the empty street. Bad luck for the folk at Tollergate. But it was always bad down there. He'd take the back road, he decided. Lucky he'd got the land-rover, tonight.

The water in the side-gutters now had become a white torrent and flooded in slow waves down the centre of the street, creating little dams and fountains where bits of debris had got stuck. As the road climbed, the roar of water pouring off the hills competed with his engine. It was impossible to tell sky from land and he had the hallucinatory sense that he was passing beneath cavernous trees and peaks too high to see. That story of the 'Landmark' had taken hold of his imagination and he found himself trying to picture how it would look now in this weather. He'd have to pass the foot of the Steep on his way home. It would feel like the end of the world up there!

Of course, no one but an utter idiot would attempt to go. But something irresistible had got into his brain. He wanted to see the old inn light as travellers would have seen it years ago. In these modern days of computers and mobile phones everything seemed so certain and secure. Yet on a night like this, the forces of nature reasserted themselves with a random fury and there was something exhilarating about being swept helplessly along. He took a sharp turn left and plunged into the upper dark. Here, streams had burst their culverts and gushed directly across the road. A tree lay uprooted in the momentary swerve of his lights.

Adrenalin began to course through his blood - the same delicious sensation that had kept him all those years addicted to his bleeper and his fire boots and the first intoxicating whiff of smoke. After the initial climb, came a long, blind haul - dashes of white

40

foam - and tawny grasses, wind-flattened by the roadside. He peered straight ahead, looking for the light, which should have been his guide. Surely he ought to be able to see the pub by now. He would book himself a room, if he got there alive and telephone home that he was safe... Unannounced, the building loomed out of the dark and he had to brake to avoid it. Some idiot had changed the front.

In place of the old inn light, a banner the size of a motorway sign now straddled the entrance gate. In dimly-lit purple and orange. it read: 'Heritage Motels welcome you to the historic Landmark Inn'. He couldn't see the light because it wasn't there. An expanse of gravel led to further hoardings, depicting the delights within: en-suite showers; wi-fi internet access; Macdonald's-style hamburgers. Alf grimaced. Another pub gone forever. Inside, there was lilac carpet with matching Christmas trees. Gamma Peggy's Carvery offered as much as you could eat for £10 a head. Christmas Day Special: free chocolate mousse with every turkey dinner. The place smelt faintly of disinfectant.

A mirthless woman at the counter rebuffed his enquiry. A room? There were no rooms to let on the top floor. In fact there were no rooms to let tonight. The staff were being sent home early. The Carvery was closed. Not enough customers to justify staying open when the weather was this bad. They hadn't a hope of hitting their financial targets what with the economic recession and competition from places down in the valley.

Alf gave a snort and made as if to leave.

Suddenly she relented. "Look, love, it's a rough night, I know. I can do yer a coffee, but then I've got to get off home. You'd best do the same as well. Go and sit yerself down and I'll bring yer something over." She pointed to the lounge seating area.

"Are you always this welcoming here?" asked Alf when she arrived. To his surprise she had brought real coffee and there were cranberry tartlets too.

"Nicked them from the kitchen," she smiled. "Staff leftovers." Then, in answer to his question: "They're packing up, aren't they?"

"Packing up? But it should be a gold mine here. Everyone knows this place."

"Well it's changed hands plenty of times before. They had a huge clear out about the time I came. Before they built the motorway this was the main trucker's stop. Then the lorries went up the new road and all the trade went with them. They had to start over again from scratch. Nothing stays the same for long. But the present owners don't like it here. They're from the South. And they can't keep their managers. Ever since they took over there's been nowt but trouble and bad luck here. Someone wrote an article in the local paper saying we'd changed our name from the Landmark to the Eyesore, and now that's all folk can remember. They don't like that big sign out the front. And then there've been all those traffic accidents on the pass."

"Traffic accidents?"

"People coming off the road in the dark by the big cutting. They've put up a barrier but it happens just the same - a real black spot. Bosses' wife did it only the other week. Skidded right off the road. Though she's a bag of nerves, that one." Another gust of wind hit the windows, reminding them that if they wanted to sleep in their own beds that night they shouldn't leave things too long. "She doesn't have the stomach for a place like this."

"Doesn't it bother *you*?" said Alf. "Working so out of the way?"

"Me, love? Oh no. I'm not superstitious."

"What is there to be superstitious about?"

She had folded her arms around the empty tray and now stood hugging it flat to her chest. "Imagination!" she said confidentially. "Fancying things! We're not like that up here - not northern folk. But *her*, she'd frighten herself to death on a summer's afternoon! That room you wanted - they haven't let that out for years. *She* heard something up there once and that was that."

Alf looked on expectantly and she grudgingly continued: "Rumour has it that years ago, before my time, there was a chimney fire here and a young fireman fell off the roof and was killed. She's dead queer about that. She reckons he's still around. It's rubbish but it's got to her so bad she can't stand being in the place alone. I'll let you into a secret." She sidled closer.

Alf bit his tongue. "About the fireman?"

"No! *Fireman!*" she pulled a derisory face, then returned to her theme. "This place is really packing up. They're getting out and a millionaire chap is buying it. He's offered me a good job too - bar manageress. And it's going back to how it used to be. Retro-like. That's the new fashion now. Spit and sawdust and old-fashioned tatie-pot! People have had enough of that Noovelle Quizzine. They're going to make Gamma Peggy's Puddings again."

Alf drained his cup. "I'm glad to hear it."

"You tell your friends. They're going to put the Landmark back on the map! That is, if it doesn't wash away tonight! Which way are you headed?"

"Only a mile or so back over Brackenthwaite way. And you?"

"I've to get to Garside. But my hubby's coming to fetch me. There'll be no floods over there. No, you tell your friends it'll be all new at Gamma Peggy's and there'll be no more rubbish about bad luck. I've been here twenty years and I can tell you there are no ghosts here and certainly no old firemen."

Alf was smiling as he rose to go. If Sid's ghost could put Tatie Pot back on the menu, it was a philanthropic spirit! "You have a nice Christmas now," he said, but she was still in full flow.

"No firemen!" she called after him. "That's just rubbish they make up for the tourists. I've worked in this building half my life so I know. All you'll ever hear in the roof up there is the wind, and it doesn't sound like no fireman. It just sounds like the wind or like a little child crying."

43

Dead Letters

Dead Letters

The bungalows were built on a piece of land, listed on the archaeological survey as Ben's Field, though who Ben was, or what business he had once had there was long lost to local memory. Enthusiasts with a metal detector had once unearthed empty cartridge cases and part of a riding stirrup, and the present occupier had been dismayed to find large quantities of rusty tin in one of her flower borders, but these things apart, there was practically no sign of previous occupation. Everyone knew that the site of an old barn lay thereabouts and the 1870 tithe map showed a homestead named Long Neb, but all trace of that had vanished and when Elsie Cartright moved into her new designer home, the plot itself seemed pristine. Picture windows gave onto an uninterrupted view of the horizon's blue hill-line, and the property itself boasted the latest conveniences: a generous drive, fitted kitchen, en-suite bathrooms (*several* of them!) and real-look electric log-fires…

She and Greg quickly set about laying on the finishing touches. With his bountiful bank manager's salary and her good taste, the place soon held its own against competition from any of the well-groomed houses roundabout. And when Greg passed away, Elsie worked tirelessly to maintain everything as he would have liked. Wiry and alert, like a little bird, she did the work of several paid gardeners, and additionally oversaw the church flower committee, volunteered at the local museum and acted as treasurer for the Women's Guild. She was artistic and clever with her hands. It was she who had instigated the new church kneeler project and had put heart into the needlepoint novices of the parish, setting them stirring targets for completion and sorting out their tangles and muddles with untiring zeal. A woman of her time, assertive, unflagging, she enjoyed the respect which her well-spent energy earned her. She applauded achievement, deplored all sloppiness, so, when the post began to go astray one Christmas, she was predictably rattled.

The first card arrived with the first frost. It had been unseasonably mild all winter and two weeks before Christmas, the marigolds were still blooming their heads off in Elsie's garden. The lawns, a lush swathe of emerald green, swept away to a border of shrubs, which had put forth a confused smatter of blossoms even before they had dropped their autumn leaves. Elsie surveyed the scene with satisfaction. According to the rules of good garden design, she had arranged colours and textures, features and statements to show off the qualities of plants and gardener alike and the Japanese corner, the prairie meadow, the retro miniature conifers, a lone, life-like goose sculpture, gave witness to her annual pilgrimages to Chelsea. The garden was a metaphor for everything she prized: order, progress, efficiency...

She had collected her mail from the doormat, lost in this pleasing reverie, and wandered into the kitchen, where she could enjoy a cup of instant coffee along with the view. There was a begging letter from the Donkey Sanctuary, two unwanted catalogues and car tax reminder. She could deal with those later. The sight of an odd grey envelope, incorrectly addressed, however, sent an inexplicable shiver down her spine.

So many cards now came with printed labels, she rarely saw the hand-writing of her friends. But this, written in vintage longhand, was something she could not explain. The address was perfectly correct, but the name...

"Miss M. Tyler,
59, Barfield Lane,
Fletcham,
SUSSEX."

No post code.

Her coffee cooled while she puzzled over it.

All the business of the lane, if not of the entire village, was Elsie's business but she knew of no Tyler past or present living there. Her own family was now reduced to a few far-flung cousins and she made it a rule not to have guests to stay, so this could not have been sent for her to pass on. Her immediate neighbours were called Fanshawe, but she was in the middle of a dispute with them and had stopped speaking to them till the solicitors could come to terms. There was no way of knowing if 'Miss Tyler' belonged to them. Someone had made a mistake - acted in a hurry and created a needless muddle of the sort that wasted so much valuable time and effort.

Elsie put this mail, unopened, beside the cards and fairy lights on her long, brick mantle-shelf and went about her day's affairs. After completing her shopping, she consulted the parish clerk's wife who directed her to the post office cashier who confirmed the need for action. There were only seven days left for guaranteed delivery, so, on her return home, she crossed out the writing on the envelope and wrote above it: "*Not at this address. Return to sender.*" So far so good. But her satisfaction was short-lived. Without a sender's address, she realized, the item could not be returned, and if the envelope contained more than a card, which by its weight it *might*, then it would most likely be looted at the post office depot, and end up in the pocket of some unscrupulous employee. One didn't like to think these things... but Elsie *did* think them. Habitually.

By evening, she was still uncertain what to do and, but for the disturbances of the following day, she might have persuaded herself that she had done enough. Her conscience warmed to this possibility. If it was nothing to do with her, why should she get involved? However, Fate took a different line. If it was nothing to do with her, why were new problems already poised to provoke her?

Wednesday proved foggy and damp; the view from the French windows, half-erased. Today a busy day. There were the church flowers to do for the Children's Service at six; final preparations for the Women's Guild Christmas Tea Party (her sponge cake contribution sat neatly on its doily, ready-dusted with sugar and sealed in its festive tin) and then, mince pies at the Hansons'... Though she felt that they represented a vulgar, new element in village life, yet Elsie would be the last to stand off. Manners were manners and these public displays of wealth and influence provided a vital opportunity for gossip, which she despised, yet utterly depended on... She returned to the task in hand with an effort of will.

49

Just beyond her polyresin goose were the shrubs, variously struggling into bloom: lilac, mahonia, and the lovely, delicate pink of winter viburnum - just the finishing touch for her pulpit bouquet. Slipping on her plastic galoshes, she sallied forth, secateurs in hand and all but stepped on two large, green and white turds, about the size of her thumb. There, on *her* grass!

Looking about, she spotted more, an alarming number more. The goose fixed her with its inanimate eye. Where could the living creature be, which had produced these foul offences? Had something broken through her rabbit-proofing? Or flown in from the fields beyond? She hastened back to the house to fetch a scoop, tripping, as she did so, over something else, which had definitely not been there before: a freshly-chewed marrow-bone, of obscene proportions! Her mind recoiled from this double outrage. And who was responsible? Vermin? Vandals? Her thoughts naturally turned towards her neighbours and the ongoing dispute. Would they really be so silly as to sabotage her garden, knowing her efficiency in legal matters? For once, she decided, 'no'. Local youth? Drunken boys? One read about these things in the papers and nowadays a good address offered little immunity.

Elsie removed the debris, and dropping it into an antibacterial sack, set off for church feeling decidedly short of cheer. Though she gained some relief, throughout the day, by unburdening her feelings to others, the sight of that grey envelope on her return, stirred her to irritation once more. How she hated loose ends! A weaker woman would have succumbed to misgivings, but Elsie would not waste her time this way. Doubtless there was a normal and trivial explanation which would resolve all in the morning. Nothing could be done just now. She cast her eye appreciatively round the dust-free, odour-free, freshly-upholstered space she knew as home, with its soft-pile carpets and arrangements of potted plants, turned out the fairy lights and the spangled Christmas tree that fitted so neatly into its fireside niche, patted the lemon chair-backs, and closed the door, leaving her embroidery and Greg's paintings equally in the dark.

The newsreader the next morning announced that flights from Heathrow were suspended. Freezing fog held all of Southern

England in its grip, and a rime of barbed hoar frost fringed every bough, leaf and blade in Ben's Field.

Elsie was up and about her business early. There would be the church to clean, *inevitably,* after the carols, for the parents, who so proudly took their charges home, hardly gave a thought to the mess they made. And someone had to sweep up the crumbs and scrape the mud off the kneelers afterwards. Childlessness had left a well of pain in her heart, which had crusted over, for everyday purposes, with indignation at the thoughtlessness of others. Mothers were a particular target, with their oblivion of the world about them. But it was easy to find others: dog-owners, people who went on foreign holidays; people who parked their cars in the High Street, and those who borrowed money on their credit cards and then couldn't pay their bills on time. Some managed to be guilty of all these offences *and* commit other crimes as well... Her thoughts were arrested by the sight of another envelope in the hall. Long, slim, blue...

It read *"M. Tyler"* again, but this time in a different hand: feminine, round, almost French-looking, with fancy serifs. The envelope felt fat and smelt of cheap, old-fashioned perfume. Once more a shiver shot through Elsie's heart - the same reminder that she perhaps she could *not* arrange and organize everything in her world; indeed, that there might be whole worlds apart, which operated according to different laws and acknowledged nothing of her sense of propriety. This troubling discovery was soon followed by another.

The blue light of the frost-bound garden had taken possession of Elsie's lounge. But without so much as a nod to this or any other natural mystery, she flicked on the light. This new envelope could join the other, until such time as she could sort the matter out. As she raised her eyes she took in signs of a nocturnal intrusion which put common sense to flight, and conjured a crowd of irrational fears instead. For a moment, she was no longer the self she knew. She wondered if she was suffering from dementia. If not, she must be the victim of some ugly conspiracy, for things were certainly not as she had left them. Large, muddy paw prints led from window to sofa, where some rough-and-tumble had lately taken place. The sofa itself, in its lovely, lemon upholstery, was littered with orange hairs!

Her first reaction was to find someone to blame. Dogs, children, Christmas robbers, neighbours... She sat down with a thumping heart, thinking of the letters which had recently flowed with such alacrity between her solicitor and that of the family next door. The contention: a tree house, built in the venerable ash which overhung her garden. It had been erected without any planning or building regulations; a violation of her privacy, an eyesore and a threat to public safety. The structure was frequently full of boisterous children, with or without their pets, and since she had declared a state of war, Elsie viewed it as an enemy lookout and potential launch-site for assaults upon her property. Only the other day she had picked up a perfectly revolting wooden puppet with jointed legs made of twigs, which had fallen onto her lawn. Tempted to throw it back where it had come from, she had decided, instead, to keep it as evidence. How these muddy paw prints could be linked to the tree house she could not quite fathom out. But suspicion needs little fuel. And Elsie cleaned the church that morning with the same grim vigour she had just expended on her sofa cushions.

Guests at the Women's Guild party noted a tightness about her lips in the afternoon, yet left without discovering the cause. Normally quite busy with her tongue, she remained withdrawn, even keeping to herself the observation that some upstart had mixed bought pies with the genuine, home-baked ones. And wasn't it just a sign of how standards were falling!

She returned home heavy-hearted, apprehensive even; averting her eyes from the inflated snowmen on the lawn next door; hardly bothering, even, to articulate to herself the truism that all *that* had nothing to do with Christmas. But the old Elsie was not to give up without a fight. Anyone could face discouragement if they were strong enough. In the old days she would have looked, for inspiration, to national figures of merit. How would Margaret Thatcher respond? Certainly not by caving in!

She put on the kettle, found her reading glasses and sat down at the kitchen table to tackle the problem at once. Opening other people's letters was something she naturally considered utterly taboo, but here were exceptional circumstances - one might almost say, a state of emergency. In such a case, normal niceties were a luxury one could ill afford. She would go so far as to say: in which duty positively required a sacrifice of conscience.

As she opened the first envelope a gust of wind from nowhere rattled through the house:

"Dear Madge," she read. *"Shall be motoring down, as usual, the day after tomorrow. Hope to arrive by four if the fog is not too bad. Gus looking forward to meeting you again. He remembers your lovely kitchen from his last visit - not to mention your splendid log fires, which quite put my meagre academic rooms in the shade. Save us a good bone or two. See you soon old gal. Your loving brother, Stephen.*

P.S. I hope Ben has finished that walking stick for me. I shall need it for negotiating Sussex mud and stiles with my arthritic knees!"

The printed letter-head ran: Fellows' Lodgings, Caius College, Cambridge.

Without hesitation she broached the second envelope. This was from one Sylvie, Poplar Avenue, Pimlico.

"Dearest Aunt Madge, I can't wait to see you and all the old gang again. I'll be down on the afternoon train, 3.15, at West Barfield, so tell Cousin Stephen he can pick me up in his lovely big motor. I am trusting that this time he will leave that hound behind. It took an excessive interest in my fur coat last year. The poor thing has long since seen its best days, but I can't afford anything new until the publishers send my next advance. You'll love the new story - it's all romance and moonlight and Indian army officers. Everybody will look down their noses - except you, darling - but who cares? It pays the rent - and dreams are free. Cissy says the boys have had whooping cough. Well, well, we'll catch up on all our news over a lovely glass of sherry. Till Thursday, Yours ever, Sylvie."

Elsie laid the letter aside and stared at the deepening dusk. She was no longer sure what she thought. One moment she chided herself for going soft. The next, she felt strangely moved. By turns curious, baffled, irritated, her mind teased over the events of the past few days. If this *was* a conspiracy, it would seem to be of supernatural dimensions. The paw prints, the bone, the fox fur... Oh nonsense! She hustled herself to bed, but sleep was fitful. For the first time since she could remember, she felt vulnerable and it was an anxious woman who rose on the morrow and hurried to check the post. Nothing there. All quiet and orderly in the lounge. The garden immaculate and on this third day of frost, evolving into a crystal fantasy. Perhaps she had overreacted. Perhaps she was in need of a holiday. She had been *so* busy of late.

With her nerves still jangling, she attended mid-week communion and meekly endured a very wet sermon from the rector on caring for outcasts at Christmas. Declining several invitations to coffee afterwards, she made her few village purchases and headed for home. Yes, she needed rest and quiet. She would be back on form in a day or two and then the rector should look out and a few others, besides! Christmas was a time, not for wetness and sentiment, (the Bible gave no indication of that,) but for rising to the challenge of the moment. Mary and Joseph had done just that. You could say they were self-made people. They didn't let obstacles get in their way. You never saw Mary looking weak and feeble, like most women who had just given birth. There she was, neat and tidy, sitting up doing business with her visitors, like any well-bred society hostess. Elsie and Greg had endeavoured to set a similar example. They were busy but unencumbered. *They* had never needed others' help. Always careful with money, they had made sure that they were financially independent, paid their taxes, organized their own holidays. Why couldn't everyone be the same? They had *chosen* to live privately, but they were busy on the outside. And it worked perfectly. They had lots of interests but nothing got in the way. Pioneers, you could say. They were the first to do so many things: own a video, build a barbeque, install mirrors and metal balls in the garden... They busied themselves with projects which needed constantly to be replaced, updated, lest one got stuck, got stagnant, got bored... They had made an art of having everything ship-shape and up to date. All debts paid, all accounts settled and the rest was nobody else's business. *That* was how Christmas ought to be...

What she had not expected, in the midst of these reflections, was a telegram. The boy with the bicycle brought it after breakfast and by the time she realized that the address was wrong, he was back on his saddle and careering out of sight. Typical. Typical youth. Not listening. Not stopping to do the job properly and leaving others to sort things out. Elsie's irritation poured back, and it took her some time to recall that telegrams were a thing of the past, and that this, with its Christmas cartoon-illustrations, was an anachronism that had no place in the twenty-first century:

"COMING FRIDAY" it ran, *"WITH SURPRISE. LOVELIEST GIRL IN THE WORLD. PLEASE MAKE HER WELCOME. YOUR LOVING GODSON. NICK."*

The whole situation was becoming intolerable. Could it really be a hoax, some plot to undermine her nerves? To play such tricks at Christmas, preying on a defenceless, old woman, alone, seemed too despicable! But how else could she explain what was happening? She was not so unhinged as to think that her house was invaded by goblins! Well, whatever and whoever was behind it all, would find her a worthy match. She was ready to take them on, and her solicitor would hear of every last detail.

An escalating catalogue of 'events' confirmed this bullishness in her over the course of the next few days. There were the piles of pheasants' feathers, which appeared under the ash tree in the garden; crumbs and jam-smears on the precious sofa cushions; cigar smoke in the bedroom; a stain on the mahogany occasional table, where somebody - somebody wearing a rather exclusive scent - had carelessly spilt some nail polish remover...

The letters kept pouring in, too:

"Dear Aunt Madge, So sorry Cissy and I will be late, but the twins have had whooping cough and we can't be too careful, so will come down in stages. We are all dying for some healthy country air and the boys keep asking after Ben. Is he still living rough in that caravan in the field? Did he ever carve those puppets for them, as he promised? They speak of nothing but plucking pheasants and catching rabbits and whatever other doubtful skills he taught them. It seems they managed to understand him when all we sensible grown-ups failed. I know I was frightened of him when

55

I was a boy, but then he had only just come out of the war and was very jumpy, poor fellow. He's a harmless, decent enough chap, I'm sure, and you're a perfect dear to keep an eye on him as you do. We are in the middle of packing. Tell Sylvie - no, never mind - I'll tease her myself when we meet. Your loving Frank."

"*Dear Miss Tyler. We shall be five for Christmas if you can squeeze us in! Susan, Milly, Charlie, the baby and me. We can pick up Uncle Roger from the station. Henry"*

"*Madgie dear, Couldn't get the port after all. We'll have to rely on your sloe wine. But I'm bringing a rather nice stilton, which will go with it a treat! Bless you, dear thing. Roger"*

What was that? A door slamming? A snatch of laughter? A hibiscus blossom rudely snapped from its stem? Somebody violated the holly at the gate and tore off the boughs with the finest berries. Someone else let the milk boil over and burn on the halogen hob...

Elsie threw open the bathroom door, to find the mats all trodden askew and the tub brimming over with muddy water. Floating where it had been dropped, was a knitted cat in a blue pinafore ... she pulled it out in a rage, and then, unexpectedly crumpled. The water was still warm, still madly slopping about. The dripping toy instantly doused her skirt.

Perhaps the strain of it all was just too much. Perhaps a memory stirred of her own childhood affections. Something quietly broke in her heart and she began, through her tears, to straighten the woolly ears and paws, with a tenderness lost for half a life. After that, she found herself, like a stranger in her own house, listening at doors, prying into cupboards, anxiously inspecting the lawn for proof that that goose was alive and well! She caught the scent of scones fresh from the oven, the chink of glasses, a tumble of footsteps in the passage. All her normal preoccupations faded into insignificance. What *happened* about the twins? And the fur coat? And did Nick's girl accept when he confronted her with the flower in the hall?

On Christmas Eve it snowed. And the following morning the sun finally broke through. The whole, lovely vista of trees, melted

56

into the blueness of the hills beyond. Neighbours, who had been disturbed that night by a rumpus in the street, were doubly perturbed to note that Elsie was absent from church. They hurried back together after the service to find their darkest fears confirmed:

The neat, white gate, with its holly wreath, stood ajar and the lawn, always so pristine, was scumbled over with tracks where some recent scuffle had taken place. The front door gaped and in the hall, in the kitchen, things were jumbled here and there, spilled food and wine mingling with presents, half torn from their wrappings. No sign anywhere of the rightful owner.

As they tiptoed from room to room, Elsie's white-faced friends almost missed the two letters that were propped against a teapot.

"*Dear Miss Tyler,*" read the first. "*Save some Christmas pudding for me! I shan't be able to come too early, but will do the best I can. I've found the puppet for the twins, and a very good bottle of port (Greg **did** know his wine, if not much else!) The vicar was right, after all, it **is** good to take in an outcast at Christmas, and I can't tell you how thrilled I am to be joining you at last. Yours, most sincerely, Elsie Cartright.*"

The other, addressed to Warburton and Squeadle, Solicitors, left them equally baffled:

"*Dear Mr. Warburton, With reference to my recent correspondence re. the tree house at No. 57 Barfield Lane, please note that I would like to withdraw all previous objections and enclose a cheque in the sum of £2,000 which I would like you to forward to the occupants, to ensure that the structure is made safe for future use. Yours sincerely, etc. etc.*"

And if you would like to know whether it was the best Christmas of Elsie's life, and whether she returned a new woman, well, you will have to look her garden goose in the eye and judge for yourself whether he is now real, or not.

The Midnight Rat

The Midnight Rat

Had it not been for the rat in the night, it is doubtful that I would ever have become so involved in the affairs of Arnold Haldane. True, I have been, since childhood, a listener at doors, a collector of discarded scraps, lists, letters; one with, some might say, an excessive interest in the private business of other people. But then I have no intimate circle of my own acquaintance. A loner, me, consigned to the peripheral world of shared lobbies and visits to the public library. And I maintain I do no harm with my curiosity.

It was purely for my own comfort and amusement that I first developed the habit of spying on my neighbours, and - yes, I confess it - still continue the practice when I can, though the advent of computers and pocket telephones has spoilt the fun of the thing.

Life has changed forever, and its message is stark: change too or be damned. I can tell you there have been times when I felt I had no reason left to live. All my little pleasures being cut off, one after another. I can no longer keep tabs on the tenants by sorting their post in the hall. How should I now know whether the old man in No. 7 has heard from his daughter, or whether the actress in No. 5 is once again in trouble with her tax? They no longer have post to sort and their texts and e-mails are cruelly beyond my scrutiny. Nor can I any longer participate in conversations held at the communal payphone by my door, simply by loosening the latch and pressing my ear to the gap. The payphone has gone. And with it, the habit of calling folk just to *talk*. Twenty-five years ago things were different. Even amongst these second-rate flats and bed-sits, there was a kind of community and gratifying rewards for any with an eye for detail, a nose for intrigue and time to devote to the science of speculation. Here in the Old Town quarter of Salthaven, I swear, half the population lived, as I did, in a tenebrous world of dreams. All gone now.

Then there was room for us. Veteran survivors, with reduced but independent means, scraping along on that peculiarly English amalgam of pride and hand-me-downs... Arnold Haldane was one himself. A writer. Unsuccessful. Seedily dressed in his dirty mac. Slouching out to breakfast at Jim's Bar on the front, affecting Grub Street in his trilby hat, pockets stuffed with papers...

Only, of course, he wasn't really Arnold Haldane. The fat envelopes containing his rejected manuscripts bore that name. But his bills and junk mail were addressed to a nonentity: Harry Baines. Harry Baines had reconstructed *himself* from the inaudible parts of an imagined dialogue. Couldn't keep it up though, not even to his own satisfaction. On more than one occasion he had appeared at my door long after ten, a half-spent whisky bottle in his hand, and begged me to come up and keep him company. Me! I could have laughed. Doubtless the actress and the girl from the florist's shop in No. 2 had already turned him down. But me! A plain slab of a woman, the wrong side of forty. A woman whom nobody trusted.

"*Please!*" I remember him wheedling. "If you only knew... I'm so afraid when I'm alone."

You will be surprised at my refusal, thinking I would relish his confessions. But timid and risk averse I have always been. Laugh if you must, I could not, as a virgin, albeit a frowsty one, help doubting his motives. The sordid reality of Harry Baines sent me promptly into retreat. Besides, I did not want to be told everything straight. I wanted to infer, to surmise, to keep my own ruminative world intact.

The fact that he died so precipitately afterwards, left a sour taste, I'll allow. Perhaps a friendly confidante could have saved him from himself. Perhaps he knew what was coming. Certainly the coroner had no hesitation in pronouncing 'death by natural causes'. Well, he had abused his body for years, what with the cigarettes and the booze and there is no way you can argue with a heart attack. But to be sitting bolt upright at your work, as if you had seen a ghost... Another thought inevitably occurred to me. Perhaps he was also defeated by the sight of those packages, addressed, on his Corona typewriter, to his own sad alter ego, ('*I enclose a self-addressed envelope for the return of my manuscript*') and the unmistakable thud with which they landed, so regularly, in the hall. He would lope down the stairs and snatch them from the table where I had casually laid them: this one from London, SW1, *this* one from Edinburgh. He must have tried all the literary agents. In those balmy days, you could tell so much from a postmark.

Anyhow his going was a shock. And inevitably shrouded in secrecy. It seemed, he had no family - well, *I* could have told them that - so, after the inquest, the landlords called in house-clearers to dispose of his effects. The good stuff - not that there really was any - went to auction. The fitted furniture stayed. The remaining junk was bundled into sacks and placed by the communal dustbins.

Exit Arnold Haldane. A pity. We all, in some obscure way missed him: the tappity-thump of his typewriter on the landing; the affected boom of his voice. He was the only man I knew, who *wanted* to be overheard, as if that would prove to him the reality of his own questionable existence. His table at Jim's Bar was promptly commandeered by a surfboard salesman...

Autumn '87, it was. I remember great peach-coloured clouds, like chrysanthemums, towering above the rooftops of Winterfleet Road. The gulls winging in from the sea. I'm not poetic, but I notice things...

A parcel came for Arnold Haldane the day after they emptied his room. This one was a thumper, a whole novel by the looks. I picked it up and squeezed it in a moment of regret. And then I did an unaccountable thing. The house stood quiet - no one stirring, for the post came early on a Saturday. I tucked the parcel under my arm and took it to my room.

As I argued it to myself, the deed was an act of compassion, rather than theft. Who else would want the poor man's things? Didn't it seem a pity for all this work to be discarded with the rest? The manuscript looked grubby, scuffed where the envelope had split, and on further inspection I could see that it was badly typed, and daubed with that correction fluid, tippex. I concluded it had been sent out several times. The agent's slip noted regretfully that they had given his story careful consideration, but found it was not quite right for them. They wished him luck in the future.

It was a thriller, entitled *The Dumb Woman.*

And it stirred in my mind a fever of acquisitive thoughts. How many other novels were there mixed up with the rubbish by the gate? How many letters, diaries, jottings, which had been witness to the man's whole life, amongst the dead men under his bed?

All day long, while the pinky-peach clouds blossomed overhead, I kept a furtive watch on the lobby, but always there was some tenant slamming in or out and at last the sky went blank and the gulls fell silent and a wind picked up from somewhere and threw fistfuls of rain, like gravel, against the windows. That rain, I reflected with a savage impatience, would be collecting in pools on Haldane's sacks outside. It would be seeping into his notebooks and smudging the ink. A more violent blast sent the milk bottles rolling down the steps and lifted the dustbin lids. Tortured by frustration, I held on to my determination till dusk, then, putting a scarf over my head and crept round the side of the house. Here were the bins. My trembling fingers found the heap of sacks, undid the knots, and rifled through the contents. Here was an inevitable nastiness of bottles, cornflakes packets, something that felt like an old vest, cigarette butts, magazines - oh God! yes, by the faint light of the streetlamp - full of naked women. A second bag yielded up the smell of rotting food. A third contained paper - *this* must be the one! - paper and books, scrapbooks with cuttings in them, reams of loose typescript, jotters, and those familiar white envelopes, stuffed with their fat rejections. *This* bag I raided and like a tomb-robber, lugged my booty home.

Once indoors, the sense of triumph fading fast, I experienced a reaction of disgust. What did I think I had I done? I could almost imagine that Baines's shadow, lurking behind the curtains or crouching at the keyhole was watching me, furious, demanding the return of his things. I swear I would have taken them back too, but that the fear of meeting someone in the hall prevented me. I now know that it is a poor trick to make the weather mimic the action in a story, but at the time I was ignorant in matters of style. As the storm grew steadily worse, I only knew that it acted upon my guilt-encumbered mind with the force of a supernatural agent. From time to time I could hear the tiles come crashing down from the roof. Through the relentless roar of the wind in the trees, came a clatter of debris, whirling like shrapnel out of skips in the street or ripped from garden fences. The whole house groaned and shuddered under repetitive assaults. I took to my bed and covered my ears with blankets, believing that daylight would bring a return of reason, but dawn found Salthaven stricken from end to end. There might as well have been an air-raid. Trees lay uprooted across the roads, power lines tangled in heaps, buildings teetering, signs dangling, the pavements strewn with rubble. Newsreaders explained to a shaken populace that they had endured a hurricane. Here, at No 3, Winterfleet Road, the storm had shaken the fabric of the house, leaving a crack the length of my room which stirred like a breathing nostril. I might have been crushed alive. Four of us, tenants on this side, had been miraculously spared but were evacuated without delay and lodged in temporary accommodation until the damage could be repaired. With barely time to collect my things, I stuffed the papers of Arnold Haldane deep into the cupboard behind my bed - God forbid that the workmen should find them! - and life carried on in its inexorable way. After the builders, came the decorators and then new tenants moved in on the two floors overhead and my mother was taken ill in Ledbury. I had no time to think of Harry Baines. I actually forgot him. For years.

As I say, it was not until I heard the rat in the cupboard, that I gave any more thought to the matter. You know how it is with cupboards. One thing gets pushed in after another and whatever is at the back, mummifies like a corpse in a bog until some upheaval brings it back to light.

Now if there is one thing I cannot abide, it is a rat. When you live alone you have to deal with spiders, just as you have to unblock sinks, but a rat is not an accident of nature. A rat has a purpose. It is probably watching you. And it is never long on its own. As I lay awake in the early hours I could hear the unmistakable patter of feet behind my bed - a rustle followed by the grating of rodent teeth on wood. What was it chewing? What valuables had I stowed there, in my haphazard way?

The next day I took the brave decision to empty that cupboard completely. Out came the accumulation of twenty years' good

65

intentions: successive attempts to relieve the tedium of my life. A sewing machine and bundles of scraps of cloth, a pair of walking poles, boots, an electric waffle-maker, Christmas fairy lights (no longer in working order), tins of sprouting seeds, vinyl L.Ps, and more, amidst various bags of clothes too small to wear... Last of all, came a sack with a repellent, half-familiar look: the final legacy of Arnold Haldane.

Like evidence in court, these things testified against me, holding a mirror to my unsuspecting face. Twenty years ago I had joined the Ramblers Club, I had taken up patchwork quilting, discovered the power of vitamins. None of it lasted, of course. And twenty years had not improved life for a margin-dweller like myself. There were times when I felt lonely and low beyond endurance. I watched too much t.v. Ate too much chocolate. Adopted a bench on the seafront, and sat there in the afternoons, just by the iced-sugar-biscuit of a bandstand, watching the foreign students come and go... Bought myself lottery tickets, but never won...

Such reminders of former times, caused brief hilarity, then flung me into a depression which lasted for days. I found no sign whatever of the rat. And when I recovered the will to live, I made a new resolution. I would change my miserable destiny once and for all. Have my hair dyed at that stylist's on the corner. Take a course with the Adult Education. Buy myself a laptop. I would not die a sad, derelict creature, like Harry Baines. I would *become* someone. First rid myself of all that smacked of failure.

His ghost for a start.

All the same, I found myself sifting through his files, looking for anything that might redeem his memory. The indignity of his existence seemed so familiar. Here were scraps of shopping lists, betting slips, one-line observations scribbled on envelopes. Endless plottings. Character profiles. Obituary cuttings. Here were folders full of soiled typescripts, draft copies and used carbon paper. You had to admire the sheer perseverance of the man. But he had had some successes. He had written a regular column for *the Greyhound* and in 1967 he won a competition: 10 shillings, first prize, for a story in *The Gazette*. Here was his photo, smiling askance to emphasize his jaw, and a flattering biography: "*Mr.*

Haldane lives at Salthaven, the South Coast resort that is home to so many writers and artists..." In those days he had looked almost presentable.

As for *The Dumb Woman,* it ran to 600 pages of grunty, sweaty prose in cryptic sentences. There were two corpses on page one: one badly mutilated - a girl in red lipstick and a down-at-heel wrestler called 'Muscles'. There was a lot of slang about guns. Six hundred pages! It was more than I could pitch through. I tossed the work aside and settled for instant noodles and a hospital t.v. soap.

Next day there occurred another of those accidents of fate which seem to dog my life. In the hairdresser's window, I noticed an advertisement for a Women's Writer's Circle. '*Bring along a sample of your work. Make friends and improve your confidence in a warm supportive atmosphere. Be brave. Release the novelist within.*' This was just the kind of thing which would send me scuttling for cover like, well, like the proverbial midnight rat. I was a lazy reader. I had certainly never had an original thought. But some dark incubus placed the notion in my head that I could access this warmth and support without having to be brave. For once in my life I had been rather clever. I already *had* a novel. I had not yet thrown it away. I could make friends and improve my confidence, by annexing Arnold Haldane for myself! I returned to No 3, past the monumental mason's and the Chinese takeaway, as though approaching a romantic assignation.

So began a strangely exhilarating episode in my life. Hair cut and dyed a striking brunette, I made my way to the hall where the writers met, feeling hardly myself at all. A thin, earnest woman with head shaved welcomed me in. There was coffee and chat; moments of exquisite self-confession and then a public reading of work. I chose that first page with the corpses, and, in an agony of self-doubt, stammered it out. It met with stupefied silence. At the end, our tutor put a lingering arm around me and confided:

"You've got some serious anger bottled up inside. It's very exciting. Thank you for sharing with us tonight. Don't hold back next time. Just let the words flow free."

Stunned by the novelty of being noticed, I set to with a newfound sense of purpose. I would not just read Arnold Haldane, I would *improve* him.

If they wanted me to be angry, I would be angry. I inserted some expletives on page three and experienced a delicious thrill of power. Struggling to correct the original script, I wrote my copy out by hand and then made a bolder decision. I would splash out; buy a computer and sign up for lessons with the U3A.

Dolores saved me a seat by her side at the following session and everyone listened as I introduced Flood, the detective, with his bottle-scar and his seedy flat in Wandsworth…

"But darling, you can't use Wandsworth these days. It's where all the best people live," objected a florid woman in a poncho.

"It's symbolic," said Dolores. "Peel away the white stucco; we've all got seedy flats somewhere in our souls, and bottle-scars on our lips." She gave me a wink and a smile. "I have the feeling there is more, much more, and darker and more daring things than Judith herself yet realizes, where this has come from…"

From week to week I laboured at the story. I bought myself racy novels and soaked up their atmosphere. I sliced into Haldane's salty prose with new interpolations.

"I believe," said Dolores, giving my shoulders an intimate squeeze, "we should try and find you a publisher. What an imagination! Behind it all I can *sense* a powerful masculine mind at work – and the sleaze… You could make an eBook!"

How I worked! Slogged on my computer. I forgot to eat, forgot to shop. Never knew who was in the house. Dolores and I would meet in 'Americano's' and go through the manuscript together over giant glasses of coffee latte. I shocked myself with my daring. I never felt more alive, more dynamic and for once I never questioned the propriety of what I was doing. I felt more at home with Flood and his cast of villains than with anyone in the real world. Real world! What kind of fantasy was that? Dolores said we are the architects of our own being. I wanted to believe her. When she suggested I was maybe going too far, I cast the criticism off. I cast Dolores off too, perhaps a little too brutally. But I didn't want her to have a stake in 'my' work.

When I uploaded the finished text just before Christmas, I kept my name out of it and used a nom-de-plume: *Arnold Haldane*. '*Congratulations!*' read the message on my screen. '*You have just published successfully.*'

Three days later, as I was finishing supper, someone knocked at my door. It had been misty all day with the foghorn sounding down in the harbour. Funny how such things simply dropped out of my consciousness while I was working. I didn't seem to have heard the foghorn for years. But the intermittent boom of it came back now, bringing a shiver of pleasure. Out there, was darkness, danger, the unmanned lighthouse, the currents round the sands; here in the horseshoe of the town, Christmas lights, streetlamps, the hazy windows of hotels. Salthaven was still a refuge for strangers.

The man on my step resembled one. Tall, dark, with a low-brimmed hat and expensive overcoat. I could not see his face.

"Sorry to trouble you," he began in a Hispanic baritone, "We ha' jus' taken the flat upstairs and we can-not light the gas. You wool-dn't by any chance be able to help?"

Now his story rang instantly false, but I was intrigued. No. 5 was a problem flat. Ever since Harry Baines' demise, they had had trouble letting it and people didn't stay. Never gave a reason. The rooms faced north so perhaps they were too dark. But since the storage heaters had been fitted, all the flats were now electric. I knew that the place upstairs had been empty for months and looking at this man I decided he would quit. I had the feeling he was simply spying.

"You with your wife?" I enquired. Two could play that game.

"With friends. Here for the Convention. It seemed too good a chance to lose, staying actually in this house." He held out a black-gloved hand.

"Convention?"

"Crimewriters! The other delegates will be arriving soon. Thanks for the matches."

The news came as a shock.

"I'm – I'm a published writer myself." I babbled, but he was already in retreat.

"Everyone has got a book!" He tipped his hat with an outmoded courtesy and backed away.

"I didn't catch your name,"

"Oh Samson, literary agent!" He smiled and vanished up the stairs.

Well, if this wasn't another of those crass coincidences! What more could a budding author hope for? In the morning I would collar Mr. Samson and plead my cause.

All evening I listened to footsteps coming and going; the front door swinging discreetly on its hinges. There were whispers, mutterings, snatches of laughter in the hall and the sound of heavy bags being trundled upstairs.

Then the music started. Jazz, it was. Started at 10 o'clock, directly over my sitting room. At first I welcomed it. It was nice not to feel so alone. But they must have opened the windows and, well, by half past two, the whole thing had gone beyond a joke.

Twice I ventured out of my door, but my courage failed me. Fred, the carpet-layer in No.1, must have been out. And most of the others had gone away for Christmas. The house felt suddenly islanded in darkness, with that enveloping fog creeping in from the sea... Layers of unreality. Where did they end? At the Chinese Chippy, which never closed? Or the funeral showroom which never opened? And beyond them? There above the banisters, the newcomers had, with some nerve I felt, already pasted a poster. But my annoyance swiftly gave way to astonishment:

'1st Annual Convention' ran the type, between a framework of red curtains - an old device but still graphically effective - 'ARNOLD HALDANE - Man of Crime. Guest speaker: Brett Samson. The Problem with Flood.' The ink had run and at first glance the word looked like 'Blood'.

What did this mean? Did Haldane already have a following unknown to me? And what did they know? Had they heard of 'The Dumb Woman'? Had they come to expose me? Or would they be grateful to learn about the archive I had saved?

From where I stood in the half-lit hall I could smell a taint of cigar-smoke. Smoking was strictly forbidden. It was written clearly in the lease. Nobody allowed smoking any more. But it would confirm Samson's need for matches. That odour of the sordid that always clung to Haldane in life, seemed to have attached itself now to his followers. They weren't straight-dealing. They weren't the kind of neighbours a decent woman would want. But then 'a decent woman'? Could I any longer call myself that? I felt my heart go cold. I was a cheat too, wasn't I? A thief. A spy. Here I was already, snooping again. I had spotted a dark shape on the landing, like the huddled form of a man's overcoat. And before I could help myself, I was climbing towards it, creeping on tiptoe. The sound of laughter burst from Haldane's flat. A woman's shriek - and raucous imprecation - so unlike Dolores' low contralto. Then came the sound of broken glass. They were having a party - a rave - and leaving their rubbish outside. This huddled shape revealed itself to be a common bin-bag, stuffed with...

Someone wrenched open the door and two men hurtled forth, dragging a third, barely conscious, between them.

"Well, he won't be talking any more tonight!" laughed one. "He's going on a little trip... to visit the sewers!" Brushing past me they plunged on down the stairs and I could not help noticing how the third man's eyes gleamed in a glassy stare and his legs trailed, twisted behind him. Out they went into the fog and I hesitated a moment. I no longer believed they were literary agents. It was clear - from my own excursions into the criminal mind - that they were here to 'do a job'. An outside gang. Most likely terrorists. Best call the police. My hand, gripping the handrail. Call them now. My heart beating fit to explode. Sweat breaking out. The thugs who had all but knocked me down had kicked aside the black bag as they passed and scattered scraps of rubbish down the stairs. Scraps of letters, scraps of scribbling... HIS scribblings, his typescript... So was Haldane a terrorist too?

"Just look what the cat brought in!" yowled a contemptuous voice and looking up I saw a woman draped in the doorway.

Arline. I recognized her at once. Arline, in her red lipstick and plunging scarlet dress. Blond hair crimped around her face. Arline before she died. Before the bullet that killed her, ripped into her throat. Even down to her matching stilettos, there could be no mistaking her.

71

So now my brain was doing somersaults, like a body tumbling downstairs, trying to work out which way was up. Perhaps there were other copies of *The Dumb Woman* and this gang had got hold of one, had got hold of the rest of Haldane's literary output. Perhaps there was an agent, after all. And he had heard of my publication and set up this fancy-dress charade to frighten or blackmail me into handing over my share of the spoils. Now I looked at them, they were *all* in fancy dress. Even Mr. Samson. No one wore those wide-shouldered overcoats any more. Haldane certainly never had one. And the stooge that they were dumping down the drain, he had been knocked about a good deal, but he wore braces - his shoes were old-fashioned brogues. And something about his face had seemed familiar. A scar, like a napkin fold, defaced his lip...

Arline held a champagne glass in her hand.

"Come on up, won't you, ducky? Join the party!" She turned on her heel. And I began to see the bigger picture. Yes, if these were common crooks and I myself the victim of a criminal plot, well, I had rights as an author, didn't I? I would play them along until I could summon help. The police, well, the police would surely help, wouldn't they? Blackmail was worse than plagiarism. The police must have to work at Christmas, too...

The room upstairs was simply full of them: A dwarf with gold eye-teeth and an ear-lobe missing; 'Muscles' I would have spotted anywhere (how did they find the actors for these parts?); Dulcie, who ran the brothel along The Shingles, looking a picture: seated with one leg slung over the arm of her chair, she was busy painting her toenails. She had wedged little cotton-wool balls between her toes and held her brush with the concentrated air of a Fabergé jeweller. Her silk dressing-gown barely concealed a body grown sallow with age.

'Bring her in, darling,' she drawled without looking up. "Let's have the whole bloody show." The gramophone groaned to a halt and someone wound it up again.

I took in the room, thick with smoke, the cocktail glasses, no detail missing, and poor old Arnold Haldane sitting, bound and gagged - a dazed look in his eye. 'Bring her in. Perhaps she can give him a hand!' A general guffaw followed.

To this day, I doubt that anyone could arrange such a pageant for revenge. I began to wonder whether Haldane had really died. Perhaps he had simply faked death as a stunt and taken his good work with him. Bribed the coroner? Perhaps this was all a hallucination of my own? An overspill of creative energy? Energy I could hardly call my own.

Someone took me roughly by the arm and led me to the table. Arnold, (no mistake, this was the man and not an actor), followed me with his eyes. And in an instant I saw the terrifying truth. This was why he was afraid to be alone, why he had begged me to sit with him at night. He was persecuted by the insistence of his own imaginings, hostage to his own fantasies. No need now to explain the whisky, the aspirins, the coronary infarct... And *I* was now hostage to them too. Small comfort to think that only metres away the world was sane and free: that Petal was still frying fish in her Chinese Chippy; that the funerary angels were keeping watch over the second hand electricals, next door. That the hotel lights, the empty shops, the station clock, the late taxis would last to see another day. I didn't believe that I could ever reach them.

Of the swarm of ghouls that filled the room, every character was a cliché.

'Show her, Jawbones. Show her what she really wants to see.' They were crowding round now with an expectant air. And someone thrust a paper under my nose. Might have been any one of the dozens that covered the desk, but it had the desired effect and Arnold raised his eyes to mine as a last appalling certainty took shape. These words are mine. This is my script, my hand, my correction. Yet no product of my mind has put them there. With a sinking heart I recognize I have not the ingenuity. No, I have to face the facts, dire as they are. And the facts are that every aspect of my life has been, from first to last a sham, a cocktail of coincidence and improbability, the fifth-rate permutations of a second-rate mind. I can no more move or scream or wave my arm than I can prevent the destiny that now reveals itself. To be condemned forever to an existence of which no word has ever been original. I *belong* to him. A hideous, hopeless creature. I am just one of any number of his *Dumb Women*! And if not his, then whose? Are we both pawns in another, unknown hand? The old hack slips his gag and blinks a smile.

"Make her read it. Let's all share the joke."

And I begin to run my course again...

"Had it not been for the rat in the night," I read, *"it is doubtful that I would ever have become so involved in the affairs of Arnold Haldane..."*

The Hand in the Fire

The Hand in the Fire

"Ditton? That you? Look, it's Trumper here. Major Trumper. What the devil is wrong with that wood you sent me? *Top quality vintage oak* - my Aunt Fanny! Damned stuff simply doesn't burn! What?" The Major held the receiver in mid-air while he adjusted his hearing aid, then resumed:

"I don't care if it came from the Taj Mahal - it's no bloody good, man! Just sits there and smoulders. And do you know what the thermometer went down to last night? Minus bloody seven. It's no joke, old love. I'm freezing my whatsits off here. You know the boiler's on the blink. I can't get a man till tomorrow and I told my log chap not to deliver because of what you promised me. Don't try to give me a lesson on laying a fire, thank you! I'm a world authority wood and I'm telling you that that stuff is no go. So what are you going to do about it?"

Muted quackings from the other end of the line.

"You will?" The hectic colour paled a little from the Major's cheeks. "Your fellow will drop off something else tomorrow? All right, but it must be seasoned. And no pine. I can't burn pine. It spits all over the carpet. I want English oak, tell him. Oak, ash, blackthorn, holly. You've got dry stuff from the Common? Good chap. Well, I'll manage as best I can till then. Any news about the Protestors? I've primed the local crime prevention officer. Did I tell you I caught one of them in my log-shed the other night? Nicking wood, if you please. Little gypsy kid - eight years old. No shoes on! They're insane, that lot. The sooner you get them all cleared out, the better. My only comfort was knowing that the blasted stuff wouldn't burn when he got it home! I gave him a fright though. Po-Po smelt him out. Damned scroungers! See you at golf on Thursday? What do you mean: '*It's been a bit wet*'? You've got to work your Christmas turkey off, haven't you? Hard feelings? 'Course not! It's just my way, that's all. How else do you get anything done?" (Bullying, the Clerk of the Council called it)

77

"Oh, and I've got the Conservation Committee coming round tonight. Should be putty in my hand."

Major Trumper lived in a dimity-white cottage at the edge of the Common, with his life's companion, Napoleon, a slavering, short-legged mastiff.

And here, with the assistance of the Griffins, a local couple who cleaned and gardened for him, he held bridge parties, chaired the local branch of the Old Harrovians and masterminded e-mail distribution for the Digbury Neighbourhood Watch.

Just now, he had a lot on his plate and he enjoyed the attendant feelings of competence, not to say power, which allowed him to view his less gifted peers with a touch of contempt. All the same, seventy-eight was perhaps old enough for living in a spot so remote. Since his election onto the Parish Council, he had found himself travelling the narrow lanes to Digbury most evenings of the week. Cataracts made driving difficult after dark and so, gradually, he was warming to the idea of moving into the village. Privately, though he'd been here a score of years and the place held fond memories of his wife, he found himself increasingly irked by the open countryside - all that life and growth, endlessly renewing itself on his doorstep, while he only got deafer and stiffer.

The fox-hunting days, when he had ridden the Common like a proper, freeborn Englishman, were long over. Then he had felt lord of the land. These days you had to be more inventive to believe you could retain any authority. These days the law was likely as not against you. The hunt had gone the way of free speech and gentlemen's clubs. These days there were damned obstacles everywhere you turned.

Old friends even declined a glass of port, for fear of exceeding the limit, driving home. And they were all suffering from one thing or another. Couldn't eat this. Couldn't drink that! It took a special kind of man to negotiate a way through. A man like Ditton, say...

As for the Common, it was now infested with foxes. Four of them he'd seen the other morning, holding a boxing match, bold as brass in the frosty bracken, their red coats flaming against the white. And at night they were at it again, filling the air with their gut-curdling cries. Mating time. Then, come spring, there'd me *more* foxes - and you couldn't even shoot them any more. Where's your gun licence? Where's your lock-up? No, it was time he got off the Common. The only ones who seemed to have the freedom to do as they pleased there were the 'Friends of Digbury'. *They* could set up camp wherever they fancied and enjoy the full protection of the police. Squatters! And criminals too!

The Major felt the saliva flow into his mouth. Two centuries ago he could have spat into the fire with impunity. Today he had to curb the desire. He stomped to the kitchen to make tea. Everything neat, ship-shape and scrupulously clean. From his window he could actually see the protestors' placards stuck along Ditton's fence. "No Fracking at Digbury", "Earth Shakers Go Home!", "Say No to Fiery Water", "Frack the Prospectors, not our Common!" He would die rather than admit that he felt threatened by them, but the boards looked like dirty washing, or fly-tipping out there and he found them offensive - doubly so, when he remembered that they had the nerve to send their offspring pilfering.

Once more, he pictured in his mind the pinch-faced boy he had startled, only the night before; noted his homespun cap, and jerkin; the defiance in his eye and the way his blue hands trembled. He had telephoned the police and lodged his complaint as soon as the brat ran off. A description would go out by e-mail that very day. He'd see to that, no matter how awkward it felt, peaching on a child. Yet, despite his righteous indignation, he had felt a shiver of regret. At Christmas time, there was something uncomfortable about people not having a proper roof over their heads. If minus seven felt cold in the cottage, it must bite a good deal harder in that makeshift protestors' camp...

The Major drilled his feelings back into line. That gave no excuse for stealing, damn it! They probably owned executive homes, if the truth was known, or flats, on benefit, at the very least. Any suffering by the squatters was entirely self-inflicted. And what about the discomfort they caused to others? He had wanted to go to his sister's for Christmas, but how could he, with that lot there, just waiting to break in?

The village stood divided about the Fracking affair. Thomas Ditton's company had bid for the land, fair and square - the Council *wanted* to sell - and the site, a mess of old gravel-workings, was earmarked for development. Ditton had promised to create two public wildlife lagoons, in return for extraction rights for gas. Who, bar a few dog walkers, would even notice what went on? Plans showed a discreet drilling rig at the injection well, with a works platform, an apron of cleared ground and collection cylinders. The company had promised to plant a screen of native hardwoods. They would create fifty jobs on site, and if all was successful, begin production in under two years.

Well we needed more gas, didn't we? Local - cheap - clean. Ditton was a decent chap, always ready to do a deal.

The whole project had all but sailed through, when professional protestors got wind of it and mounted a counter-campaign. Fracking (hydraulic fracturing of the deep earth layers to release natural gas) caused pollution, they said. Fracking contributed to global warming, lowered the water table and robbed the local rivers and streams. Pumping gasoline mixtures underground was worse. Tales began to circulate of drinking water so defiled, you could set light to it with a match - of earthquakes and dying birds. There were letters to The Times and a public meeting in the village hall. Then, one night, the 'outlanders' arrived with their travellers' vans - cut the wire and occupied the site. They parked their babies inside the entrance gates and issued a podcast, claiming brotherhood with the earth. The press made a touching story out of it.

Trumper's response was instant and unequivocal. "Shoot the lot of them!" he spluttered, dipping his moustache into his clubhouse whisky. "Set the dogs on them! That's what they ought to do!"

"I wish it were that simple," Ditton smiled back, exposing an improbably perfect set of teeth. "But I'm not without hope. Stand by me in the Council and I'll make it worth your while. We can do this all legally, you know. You help me with a right word to the right people and you won't be sorry. For a start, I'll get you all the fire-wood you need for the winter. That should save you a few bob, eh? And later there'll be shares in the company. Drink up! I'll get you another."

That was in October, and he did not question at the time, where the logs were to come from. The Common had grown in so much in the last twenty years, firewood might be cut from almost anywhere - but no, Ditton promised, this was *vintage oak.* Only later did the Major make a connection with the chapel.

The Chapel of the Hand of God had stood on the far side of the Common for three hundred years. An old dissenters' meeting house, it had been raised after the Act of Toleration and sustained by a handful of believers until the 1950s, when it fell into disuse and was unofficially taken over as a commoners' cowshed. That was in the days when commoners were a force to be reckoned with and paid a yearly rent to the reeve for grazing rights. After the cows went, the 'Hand of God' was boarded up. Various people, since then, had had a shot at restoring it, but their attempts always foundered one way or another. Even when property prices shot up, developers felt that there was a jinx on the place and nobody bothered about it till Ditton acquired it as part of his 'deal'.

Suddenly *everyone* needed to save the chapel. Experts appeared with a deluge of history and local lore: tales of Roundheads and Squatters and public execution; then the Great Storm, the demise of the Judgement Oak, a Gin Battle with the Excise... a rally of Suffragettes...

Ditton found that he had an ace in his hand and he knew just how to play it. He would restore the chapel, he pledged, and open it, free of charge, as an Information Centre, celebrating Digbury Common, all the way from the gallows to the gravel pits! He would even throw in the spot where the infamous oak once stood.

Genius!

Who could accuse him of profiteering after such an act of generosity? And who would be able to argue, if the Crown Commission surveyor condemned the roof and most of the structural timbers and declared that they must be renewed? Before anyone knew what was happening, Ditton had ripped the guts right out of the place. He got a five figure sum, in advance, for the stone roof tiles and a salvage company stumped up handsomely for the

81

doors and the gallery pews. Some beams went whole. Others had to be hewed out piecemeal and were fit only for burning. But what a windfall - the best firewood, mark you! And they would make useful bribes to friends for favours rendered. The refurbished chapel, when it was finally unveiled, would meet all modern requirements - a perfect blend of ancient and contemporary design.

Ditton had honed his plans so carefully, he hardly registered Trumper's complaint about the logs. The old boy must have let his shed get wet. How could anything be amiss with them?

But for Trumper the deal had brought nothing but trouble. He had just poured his tea, when Peter Griffin knocked at the door. The Griffins came twice a week, on Tuesdays and Thursdays, as a rule. A loyal, if rather dim-witted couple, they would willingly turn their hands to any task, if only (he did not delude himself) because they hoped to be remembered in his will. But today the man stood on the back step, twisting his face, his long hands pulling his jumper.

"Just thought I should let you know," he mumbled. "Marilyn says she's sorry but she won't be able to come today. She's had a bit of a turn."

"A turn? Nothing serious, I hope."

"Can't quite get it out of her." His hair was going prematurely grey. "She says something upset her when she was here the other day. She's not herself at all."

Trumper went on echoing like a fool. "Something upset her?"

"Round the back. You know, she's always been that way. Sensitive. Nervous, like. It's happened before. She saw something round the back of the house and it's given her the spooks. Know what I mean?"

"Not in the least." The Major hardly concealed his irritation. He had been relying on Marilyn to give the place a dust and put out cheese and biscuits for the meeting that night.

"Well, it would be out by the log store, I reckon. She won't say more."

"She didn't say anything to *me*. I was here all day. So was Po-Po. *We're* all right." A thought struck him. "You don't mean she's afraid of those travellers, do you? No need for that. I've been on to the authorities. There'll be no more trouble there."

Griffin shook his head.

"I really couldn't say. Present or past, she sees more than most people. I just know she's not up to coming out."

Trumper narrowed his eyes, recalling a moment's awkwardness with her. He had been boning up for the Committee, asking about the Chapel and the Judgement Oak. He wanted to be ready, certain of his facts and the authentic, local view was just what Marilyn, born and brought up in the village, would be able to provide. To his surprise, she tried to change the subject. And when he tried again:

"What about the Poor Man's Commune of 1650? There was a hanging or something here. Surely you know? Before the smugglers took over the common road? Isn't there something about a sunken holloway? The Local History Society gave a talk..."

"There are lots of tales," she dodged. "Most of them made up stuff. People will say Oliver Cromwell stopped in a house if they think it will sell it."

"But the Digbury Simples. *They* were real enough. You must have heard something about them. Weren't they forerunners of the dissenters who built the chapel?"

He felt he had a right to know.

"Wasn't it *their* leader who was hanged, for taking firewood off the Common and digging up the land to grow his beans?"

Marilyn had turned to face him, like a witness in the stand.

"There are many things, my mother always said, that should be left alone. And things buried deep that ought never be disturbed. I don't believe in raking up the past - not like they want to now."

"Why, my good woman, it's *history* - it's our heritage!"

"It'll bring up poison," she said and went out to the logs.

The Major blustered a way out of his defeat.

"Of course, if she's poorly, I'm sorry to hear it. Damned nuisance - nerves. Well, can't be helped. *You're* staying, aren't you? We could start on those apple trees."

"Ah!" said Peter Griffin. "I was thinking we could do that next time, maybe." A muscle twitched in his cheek. He had tucked his hands, defensively under his arms. "Marilyn's asked me to get back prompt, you see."

"Oh well, if that's the case, then you must go. Po-Po and I can manage. Give her my regards and so on. I'll see you Tuesday."

Griffin nodded and made his escape.

Fools! Thought Major Trumper. *They needed the money. They were always complaining about the rent and the expense of getting their son through college. Then they cried off over a fit of the vapours.* All that nonsense had knocked his purpose out of his head. Of course, he had wanted Griffin to fetch more logs. Now he'd have to do the job himself. He did not want to risk it later. Stupid though it sounded, he had a sinking dread of meeting that urchin again in the half-light.

Old wives tales and village gossip, *that* was what was wrong with Marilyn Griffin. All the same, it could be a bit creepy, living in the last house in the lane...

Well, he would slip out for the afternoon. It would be warmer and jollier at the bar of 'The Half-Anker", and after a pint there, pumping the landlord for tittle-tattle on the 'Hand of God', he might call into Hartgate Library and mug up on the official account before he had to face his village worthies.

By 4 p.m. he felt he was getting the picture nicely. The Digberry Simples had been a heretical sect who, refusing to go to church, had set themselves up with squatter's rights on the Common. All this, during Cromwell's Protectorate. They claimed they were the children of God and not beholden to any earthly king. They foreswore drinking and dancing and shared the little wealth they had with one another, freely. Rumour had it that they shared their women, too. They built a settlement of wattle huts, bought themselves a hand press and printed a manifesto of their beliefs entitled, *'The New Law or Dispensation of Simple Folk'*. They even sent copies to London.

The *New Law* didn't last long. When the war was over and parliament issued pardons to former Royalists, the estate at Digbury was re-purchased by its previous landlord. Legislation gave him powers to act and on the first day of Advent, or so the records tell, the Squire's bailiff, together with six constables and a mob from Hartgate, rode onto the Common and turned the Simples off. They burnt the village, confiscated the press and seized what they could as forfeit for unpaid tithes. This much is recorded in the rolls. It was winter time. Cruel, hard weather. And the outcasts had neither shelter, nor clothes for the children, nor could they look for charity from neighbours. They had not even fuel to light a fire. They were set to starve by the roadside, till one of their number, a young man named 'Go Forth', unable to stand by and watch them suffer, went back in search of fuel on the Common. The Squire's men were waiting for him and he was trussed and brought up before the bench for theft - a hanging crime.

Somehow he survived, because his signature is there, with that of the other elders, in the minute book of 1703, marking the first meeting at the 'Hand of God'. He must have been a venerable figure then. His writing is virtually illegible.

Now, thought Major Trumper, with a moment's detachment, it was not just the *land* which gave rise to contention, but the *history* too. Today's Anti-Fracking Protestors claimed kinship with the Simples who had gone before them. They even called themselves the 'Digbury Squatters'. Ditton wanted exclusive rights on that term for his Heritage Centre. Both parties painted the sect as colourful and romantic figures - centre-stage puppets in a new propaganda war. In reality, the Major reflected they were probably an untouchable rabble, a queer, fanatical bunch, like other popular groups of the day: the Levellers, Diggers, Ranters, Fifth Monarchists, Muggletonians, Uncle Tom Cobley and all... Hanging was doubtless too good for them. The law had brought them round. The law was the only thing for rebels.

When he left the library it was almost dark. A thin, sleety rain drove from the north, yet he felt a reluctance to go home. Yes, he thought, it was time to move out, cut his losses and find a house in the village. He was getting old. Napoleon could hardly walk these days. The Common was no use to him any more.

The Major smiled, despite himself. *Damned dog, Po-Po! Bit of a liability - but a dog with a heart!* He committed social offences which Trumper felt his neighbours fully deserved and which, since he could not do such things in person, he witnessed with delight.

Who trampled on Mrs. Bessamer's tulips? Who left sticky slobber on the curate's wife's skirt? Who blew off terrible farts during the village Conservation meetings?

"Oh, that'll be Po-Po. Sorry. He does a lot of that, these days. Old age!"

Po-Po also did whoopsies on the Clerk of the Council's lawn. Solid as a pig, immutable and deaf, he had eyes only for his master and his master returned the adulation in kind.

"Damned fine brute. Nothing gets past *him*, you know."

Po-Po snored, with his underbelly grossly exposed, showing a contempt for others' feelings which warmed the Major's heart.

"Po Po's the chap. He'll sort them out!"

Sure enough, on his return, he found Po-Po at the door, waggling his bottom in welcome.

"Tea first and light that goddamn fire."

The Major set his security lights, drew the curtains and checked his phone. There were two messages: one from Ditton to say would he like a grouse? A golfing chum had been on a shoot in Scotland and had come back with too many; then the Churchwarden, huffing and puffing: Mrs. Bessamer had caught the 'flu and Dr. Beaufort was still at his son's in Swindon. In view of the heavy frost predicted, would the Major mind if they postponed the Conservation meeting until next week?

The Major thought it a poor show. He had been rather relying on having 'company' that night. Even the queenly Mrs. Bessamer would have done. The more cars he could muster in the drive, he reasoned, the safer he would feel. Now, the evening yawned - a vacuum. No decent telly. He could not be bothered with dinner. He re-laid his kindling and put a match to the fire in a second attempt to burn those beastly logs. As the pine splinters sputtered beneath them, his scaffold of dried hazel prunings teased out tongues of flame and the charred remains of yesterdays beams began to smoulder afresh. He poured himself a whisky to help the tea go down.

Several hours later, Po-Po woke him with a howl. He had no idea of the time. The power had gone off, but he could see the dog's silhouette, clearly outlined before the fire. The beast stood

86

cringing and snapping at the hearth, ears laid flat against his head; the short hairs on his nape, roached up like a fin. If he had possessed a tail, which he did not, it would have been firmly tucked between his legs.

The fire must finally have taken and burnt out while the Major slept. Now it glowed, an intricate mass of embers. Needed making up.

But whatever was wrong with that dog?

He was whimpering now, paddling with his front paws, heaving his body weight from side to side, while his breath laboured in fits and starts.

There, in the grate, lay the mummy-shell forms of the logs which had burnt, momentarily preserved, before they crumbled to dust. As God was his witness, the Major saw the figure of a hand amongst them, skin peeling in ash-flakes where the hearth coals cooled.

"Po-Po, don't be such a damfool!" He lunged forward, grasping for the poker. *Knock the thing out quickly.* It brought back ugly memories of his soldiering days. Things he had seen in Korea. And the room felt cold as ice. He had candles in the kitchen. It crossed his mind that the protestors might have tampered with his power supply. If they had... well, that would certainly be the end of them. He'd have their hides in the morning, one and all! But such fighting bluster hardly helped him now.

He had the vile sensation that he was not alone and Po-Po knew it. The hound had followed his master through the hall and now stood behind him, grinning, with trembling lip.

The Major lit a taper and struggled onto a chair, but the fuse box seemed to be in order. Power cut then. But why, for heaven's sake? The weather, far from blowing up, as predicted, remained quite eerily still. An owl called. Peering through the window, he noted that all was dark at the protestor's camp. Ditton's wiring must have cut out, too.

It was only then that he spotted the other lights, far out, on the Common. Two or three, dancing about. No, four. Then none. Then two again. The buggers were up to something. Up to no good, that was for sure. He'd ring Ditton. He'd... *Blast!* He cracked his knee on the cupboard door. Oh, what was the use? *He* probably wouldn't turn out. Too busy filling his guts with Christmas grouse. He'd damned well go himself, then.

Grabbing torch and stick, he threw on his cap and jacket.

"Coming boy?"

Po-Po snarled at the door.

"Get out of the way then!"

In a fit of rage, he kicked the dog aside and flung out into the dark. Turned to lock the door, flashed his light around, and narrowed his gaze to the point where the horizon should have been. At the garden gate he paused. From here the Common stretched away in silence. Cold cut to the bone.

An inner voice began to hector him:

What was he doing, staggering out alone? Him? An old man past eighty?

Defending his property, he briskly countered.

Across the Common? Call the police, if you like...

The police were no damned good. They'd been having cups of tea with the squatters. Besides, shining a light was not in itself an offence.

So, why was he here, then?

To fend... to fend some evil off: whoever, *whatever* was creeping about in the dark - naked children, women in outlandish clothes... His frozen fingers tightened round his stick.

The lights flickered, blue, then white, between the branches, out beyond Ditton's fence. He could not see the fence itself but the land was different there. On the excavation site, where work had laid the subsoil bare, yesterday's puddles gleamed under a fitful moon. Out where the scrub grew, it was harder to see. All black, save for these dancing points... There they went again... Five this time, winking and bobbing about.

Perhaps some idiot was letting off those Chinese New Year lanterns - paper balloons with candles in them, which had become all the rage, of late. Damned menace *they* were. Made no end of mess. They'd found some caught up in the trees at the golf club once... God knows what would happen if you had a thatch!

Now the lights moved towards the Chapel and, cursing and stumbling, the Major followed after. Should have brought Po-Po. Those foxes were mating again. Their shrill, protracted scream and juddering after-moan jarred every nerve, while the half moon quietly slipped behind a cloud.

And it was near impossible to keep one's bearings. Was the path here, or there? The old boy staggered cross country while confusion and cold sent shivers through heart and head. Afraid? Who said he was afraid?

A flare appeared ahead, wafting along like a runaway plastic bag. It was nothing man-made, after all, he decided: only a phantom miasma, a trick of the brain.

Nonetheless, he splashed on - tore his face on a bramble - dropped his torch, swore and turned about. Better go home. He was getting too old for such capers. But the howling started again. Close by, this time, and so human in tone, it fairly jellied his blood. A long, intolerable wail, and sobbing - dying sobs. He could hear the air whistling back into depleted lungs; *feel* the shudders which followed... Surely, that was the sound of a man - a man, demented by pain and fear, as if his soul was being sundered away. And out there, with him, around him, these foul, unnatural lights!

His senses began to spin. Dark shapes bumped against him. Unseen fingers touched his scalp. He whirled around, flailing with his arms, trying to beat them off. As the moon sailed clear again he saw rise up before him the mass of a stricken oak, and something else besides - but before he could tell what it was, his own voice split the air.

They heard it in the protestors' camp - the scream of a man at bay. Someone was in trouble. Someone had been attacked or fallen into a pit... The young men grabbed their torches, the women found blankets and they set forth in a body, with two of their dogs, calling aloud together: "Hullo there! Can you hear us? Anyone there?"

The Major gave them a fright when they stumbled across him: frozen like a cataleptic, eyes staring wide, his white hands crossed on his breast.

They rubbed him and checked his bones, breathed life into him and soothed his gibbering with words of comfort. Then they wrapped him up and bundled him back to the camp where they brewed hot tea with honey and cayenne in it.

The children crowded round. Someone suggested an ambulance, but Major Trumper would have none of it. He clutched their hands like a drowning man.

"All right now," was all he could say. "We'll all be all right. Get along home in a minute." At that he passed out and they phoned the surgery.

When he next came round he was in his own dimity, white bed with the sun streaming in at the window. Marilyn Griffin had set down a tray. Boiled egg and fingers of toast. Tea.

"You've had a queer do," she said, smoothing his covers.

"Yes." His answer sounded mechanical.

"Not to worry now. It was lucky for you that you were found, though. Minus seven again this morning. Turned freezing after midnight. You'd have been a gonner, you know, if you'd stayed out."

"Marilyn," the Major mastered his embarrassment. "Was it you who brought me here?"

"Oh, dear me, no! That was the squatter folk. They took you back to their camp and called for a doctor and that nice young locum recognized you at once and give us a call to look in on you in the morning. They just about saved your life, I reckon. But whatever were you doing, going out there in the dark?"

"What?" He had been miles away. "Amnesia, I should think." But something was coming back. "Where's Po? Is the old boy all right?"

Marilyn straightened her apron and fiddled with the curtains. "Oh don't you worry about *him*, Major. You just concentrate on getting well."

She could not at this point tell him what had happened. How the rescue party had discovered that damned fine beast stretched out, stiff as a board behind the door. Had to break their way into the cottage, they did. Napoleon had suffered an apoplectic fit and sadly passed away.

"Silly old sod," mused the Major, forgetting that there was a lady present. But then he roused himself. "Marilyn, Peter said to me yesterday that something had upset you."

"Did he?"

"Don't prevaricate. I need to believe I'm not going out of my wits. Tell me, please - if only to humour me. *What* was it you saw that shook you up?"

She tried to brush him off. "Just someone standing by the logs. That's all." And since he was not satisfied with that. "A *man*."

"Someone stealing?"

"I'd have said *looking* for something. I couldn't really tell. He didn't stay there long."

"You could have said..."

"And worry you to death? You out here all on your own. What do you think I am? It wasn't like that anyway. He wasn't a normal man. I get a feeling about people, you know. This wasn't a man you could recognize, as such. It was a figure in a bloody shirt, and..." She sucked in her cheeks and turned away.

The Major tried another tack.

"*Tell* me about the Simples, then." He was almost pleading. "You and I - we *know* something, don't we? Richard Go Forth didn't hang, did he? What happened? Legend says that the lynch-rope broke, but there's more to it than that. *Something...*"

Marilyn sat on the edge of the bed and looked him in the eye.

"All right, if you're so sure. But it's not a nice story and I don't like telling it. I had it from old Margaret Lacey. I used to clean for her, you know, when I was a girl. Well, her people were chapel people. They'd been in the village for hundreds of years."

The Major sat up, livid-faced.

"The Civil War stuff - most of it's true enough. The tale of the the Judgement Oak dates from that time and legend says there was a hanging there. After the Battle at Hartgate, the Royalists were on the run. Groups of local Roundheads went berserk, smashed up the churches and hunted fugitives down. The generals wanted their prisoners taken alive, but feelings here were running too high for that. No one could forget the wrongs that had been done on the Common. The theft of land that had once belonged to the poor and been their home and livelihood and more. What would become of the broom makers and the basket makers and a dozen other trades besides? No one could forget that when they stood up for themselves before, the rebel leaders went to jail. Hanged and quartered they were and the Squire of Digbury was remembered as the man who pursued them to the gallows. Well, the sly, old fox paid for it soon enough. As I said, after Hartgate Battle, he was seen heading out towards the spot where the king oak grew. Never appeared again and it was believed he fell foul of a summary court and was hanged there without a trial. Not that anyone owned up or was ever called to account. But the oak got the name it was famous for. And that was the end of that, or so people thought. Squire Digbury's son escaped, up north, and well..."

"Go on."

"...the Common went back to the people for a time. That's when the Digbury Squatters arrived. But after some years, there were pardons given out. The old aristocracy returned. And when their former lands were restored, well, you can imagine there were scores to settle. The new Squire wanted to continue the Enclosures which his father had begun. And, like him, engaged the law as a tool of power. Though they had abjured all violence as sin, he blamed the Simples for his father's death. It would be a positive pleasure to destroy them. He ordered his henchmen to go with dogs and drive all trace of them off the Common. And when Richard Go Forth was arrested for theft, he avenged himself some more.

Hanging's too good for him, he thought. *His kind hanged my father. I learnt another way, in Derbyshire, that was better for a thief. If a miner there is caught, stealing lead for bullets, they make an example of him. Pin him fast by the hand, they do - drive a knife in to the hilt and leave him to his fate. I'll spare* **this** *devil from hanging and teach him a lesson too. He's a carpenter, by trade. Very well. We'll nail his hand to a tree and he can choose to work himself free or die. I know the very tree for the job: the Judgement Oak will see justice* **properly** *done."*

She had hit her stride and the Major sat open-mouthed, not so much at the tale, as at the fluency with which she told it. He had known the woman for twenty years and never yet heard her say anything of note. Could it be that he had never really *listened* before? Or was she, in some obscure way, delivering the voice of the dead, as she tapped into old Sarah's tale?

"Go Forth was twenty-five," said she, "...a strapping chap, with a wife and family. A rock of faith. Fearless in action. The very stuff good martyrs are made of. But somehow his strength and courage failed him just when he needed it most. After the sentence was performed, the spectators drifted home, but Go Forth could not tear himself away. And the longer he lingered, the weaker he became, till friends were certain he was going to die.

"At length, unable to endure the shame, he called for an axe and with his one good hand, it is said, he hacked his way to freedom...

"As for the landlord, however, he never slept again. All he could hear, whenever he closed his eyes, were the pitiful cries of the condemned and the words he had spoken to the crowd: '*It is the Hand of God which will decide the law and he who has taken that which he should not, will be judged before the Almighty and repent.*'

He tried travelling, and drinking, and whoring, but nothing would silence that voice. He grew thin and old before his time, until at last he could bear it no longer. He broke down and promised to reform his heart. That very night a great storm wrecked the country and the Judgement Oak on the Common was torn in two. Down fell the hangman's limb, and half the trunk, revealing a rotten core. And there, in the cavity, still in his battle dress, they found the corpse of the missing Squire. He had not been hanged at all, but had climbed the tree in his haste to escape, and slipped and tumbled inside. For years, the tree had been a living tomb. The skeleton's neck was broken.

"Straightaway, the Common was given back to the people. As for the dissenters, they were promised land on which to build a chapel and as much timber off the estate as they required. The Judgement Oak was naturally thrown in, as if that would buy a soul's salvation!

"So, that's how the chapel was built. They took up the boughs of that wicked tree and they turned them into rafters."

93

Major Trumper pushed his egg away. Suddenly he had lost his appetite. *What was it that carpenter fellow said? 'The Hand of God will decide the lie of the law...'*

He could hear Ditton at his elbow, now: *'We can do this all quite legally, you know...'*

Damned liar! *Vintage oak!* He was implicated in the business, up to his neck... free firewood, free grouse, free shares...

But Marilyn had risen to her feet and was staring down at him. He looked shaken and vulnerable. Perhaps he was still afraid.

"By the way," she reassured him, "what you saw last night wasn't ghosts, you know. It was what they call photon emissions. The fracking operations must have set them off. Those protestors tried to warn about it, but no one listened. They say the Council didn't want to know. Well, I had an e-mail from my son this morning. He's studying Earth Sciences, you know, at Exeter. He's taken quite an interest in all this. If you break up rocks deep underground you can release more than just household gas. Methane, for instance, can trickle out through a fault. You only need a bit of rotting weed, a bit of phosphine and you've got natural combustion - will-o'-the-wisps. That Squatter chap was cock-a-hoop. Says you did them the best turn ever, showing them where it was happening. Now they're going to test the groundwater - they reckon it's full of benzene, likely as not. It will mean the end of fracking here. And I can't say I'm sorry. What they want is starter homes for the young. My brother-in-law drives a digger for a developer who's desperate for the land... Do almost anything to get it, I reckon."

The Major was not listening. He heard himself murmur a regret - *too bad, upsetting the foxes* - but he was remembering something else. Something she had said earlier about disturbing things, digging deep...

Yes, he must get out. Get a long way away from Digbury and stay away for good. He felt a bit nauseous. Better sleep now. Make a new start later...

Marilyn took his tray and went down to begin her chores. First rake out the ashes and lay in a new fire. Thank heavens, the man was coming to fix the boiler today. These ashes got everywhere and made a home so dirty. She'd put them in the bin by the gate. Oh, but it was a bitter wind blowing off the Common today. Po-Po wouldn't have liked that. The house felt curious without him. As she emptied her can, something metallic fell out and she felt her nape go cold.

It was a rusty, hand-made nail of monstrous size. One end had been hammered over. A huge, great, ugly old thing. Whatever had the Major been doing with that?

The Horse Rider

Reader's Note

*The labyrinths of Balkan history are more complex than the
caves of Rhodope, so strangers in either may expect to lose their
way. Here are some facts, however, which I believe to be true:*

*The Rhodope Mountains, which lie on the border between
Greece and Bulgaria, are home to some of the most dramatic
caverns and river gorges in the world, including the famous
'Devil's Throat Cave', by which Orpheus is said to have entered
the Underworld. The region is rich in customs and folklore, dating
from ancient times.*

*Repeated waves of conquest and rebellion have brought Turks,
Greeks, Russians, Bulgarians and Serbs to bloody blows across the
centuries. The Macedonian-inspired uprising of 1903 was one in a
series of failed bids for independence which resulted in further
repression.*

*Once heard, traditional Bulgarian songs for unaccompanied
female voice cannot be forgotten. Their raw harmonies and
haunting measures speak, with an unearthly eloquence and beauty,
of an archetypal struggle for survival...*

*Twigs of Cornelian Cherry will blossom if brought indoors in
winter.*

The Horse Rider
Rhodope 1903

When Anelia had thrown her corn to the geese, she set her bucket on the ground and looked up. There would be a powerful frost tonight. The topmost twigs of the alders glowed pink and gold in the sun, but dusk here in the valley was only moments away. The birds knew it. There were dozens of them, just now, flitting from branch to branch, breast-feathers puffed out, hunting for a last morsel to eat before night set in. And what a night! The twentieth of December, St Ignatius' Day. The beginning of the New Year.

All the magic of Christmas began on this day. From here, where she stood, she could see the river tumbling away northwards to the free country of Bulgaria. At her back, the indigo shadows of the mountain, her father's farmstead, straddling a hump of rocky ground, with frost-covered roofs showing between the trees and all the other farmsteads of the village clustered nearby, for no one ventured far from the safety of the village - there were too many wolves and too many Turks and too many demons amongst the caverns of Rhodope.

The geese came down to the river in daylight, but now she would drive them back to their wooden shed. Yes, this day was so important. The fate of the whole year hung upon it. Early in the morning, before sunrise, they had swept the chimneys and flung the soot across the yard to protect themselves from fleas. Then her mother had baked the little ring-shaped loaves which symbolized the circle of the year and which she pressed, still warm, into their hands for them to keep till the first of January. Even the chickens had their own ritual feed of scented corn and the cattle their chestnuts. Everything must be done just right to bring prosperity and health. To make a mistake now would be to court disaster. And heaven knew, disaster was no stranger in this country. Stefan had mopped out the blood from the pig-killing. Naturally they saved what they could, but some inevitably got spilt and the water had now frozen in a glassy sheet. The pig meant the end in sight of the long Lenten fast before Christmas. A cause for celebration. So far all the preparations had gone well.

Best of all, Marko had been their 'poleznik', their new year's stranger, knocking at the door before breakfast to come and help with the pig. Marko, with his curly, black hair and his eyes like glittering coal, the straightest, handsomest youth in the village, strong, brave, secret; Marko was *her* boy. He wasn't like the others. His people had come from Rumelia, after the massacres. They didn't own land of their own and they had died when Marko was still a child, so now he was all alone in the world, hiring himself out to farmers who needed extra help. But his eyes sought out her eyes whenever they chanced to meet.

Didn't he wait behind for her, every Sunday after church, and bring her *silivriak*, the little pink-belled flowers that grew high up on the rocky outcrops? Didn't he tell her stories about far off places, and forgotten heroes? About Grandmother Eurydice who stepped on a snake and died? Her husband had tried to fetch her back - nearly succeeded too - went all the way to the Underworld and sang to the ghosts in Hell. He even sang to the wild beasts of the mountain, so great was his longing. But death was death - too smart, to be cheated by the lyre of Orpheus. There were vipers in the meadow *here* in summer. You had to be careful...

Marko had an endless fund of such stories. Yes, he was hers. Nobody knew it yet. But hadn't he put his arm round her after the harvest dance and walked her into the shadows and kissed her? When she got her Christmas bread this year she would put some under her pillow and then she would dream of him and *know* that they would marry. And Marko would be chosen to lead the carol-singers in next year's *koledari* procession. She was sure of it.

Anelia shooed the last of the geese into their hut, hung up her pail, pulled her jerkin tight and picked her way across to the stone steps of the house. Her fingers ached with cold, but she tonight she did not care.

This year, the fear that haunted her might depart. This year, she might bring herself to speak, to sing even with the others. For since she saw that terrible thing in the village she had quite lost the will to sing. She had only to see a man on horseback and she would turn to corpse-meat inside, believing the nightmare would return. Everyone said it was just a Turk. Turkish soldiers with bright swords, doing unspeakable things - that had been commonplace in Rhodope, in living memory. But Anelia knew it was the Devil. Death himself. They would need all the good luck in the world to get through another year. And good luck was brewing on Grandfather Hristov's farm this Christmas.

Four days later everything changed.

No one could tell why. Perhaps there had been a mistake. Perhaps the *budnik* - the log, which was to warm their Christmas hearth, had touched the ground when Nicolai cut it early that morning and carried it home on his shoulder. Perhaps someone had miss-said a word in the prayer that welcomed him home. Such things could spoil the best magic and turn it sour. That was why one had to pay attention to the smallest details.

In this country you could not trust politicians to bring prosperity. Politicians had a fatal talent for making the wrong alliances, promising the impossible and then signing away their dreams in humiliating defeats. Who paid? Why the people, of course. Anelia had heard the old women in the village talking; women who remembered the last in a series of wars. How the Russians had made the difference. How they had suffered and buried their dead, struggled, battled and won, celebrated independence, hoped for freedom and lost it all through a treaty in which the Bulgarians had no say. What was Berlin? Where was it? Nobody here knew. But they knew that they were given back to the Ottomans, like lambs at Easter. No. One could not trust politicians.

People who lived on the borderlands would have the shadows of Hades always under their feet. The ground might open up at any moment and engulf them. The allies of today would prove enemies tomorrow. And who were you, anyway? Macedonian, Greek, Bulgarian, Thracian? That was why one needed St. Mary, in the little gilded sanctuary in the church; the candles, the incense, the holy words to ward off evil. And that was why, for good measure, they kept to the old ways too: blessing the cattle with cornel twigs, kneading the Christmas bread a certain way. For human danger

102

was warm and red, like the pig's blood. But there were other, darker terrors abroad that went back to days before the Turks, before Alexander; days when gods like crabs walked the earth and vampires flourished to suck men's souls down to Hell.

On Christmas Eve the magic needed to be strongest of all for soon would begin the twelve 'dirty days' of Christmas, when ghouls and demons roamed abroad. Baby Jesus lay somewhere at the heart of it all, but the magic worked through other things: preparing the dishes for the final meal of the fast; spreading straw under the table; hiding a lucky coin in the Christmas dough. Anelia and the young women of the house had put on their best clothes in the morning and plaited pretzels to give to the carol-singers, and she had made one for Marko that was as beautiful and intricate as the love in her heart. This year Grandfather had invited Marko to spend the evening with them, for he had no proper place of his own to go. And Marko had promised to bring the walnuts for fortune-telling when the family feast was over.

But something had happened to Marko during the last few days. He laughed still with his lips, but his eyes shone hard and cruel and whenever he thought he was alone, he set his jaw and furrowed his brows in a frown. Anelia watched him in dismay. This man had no secret smiles for her, no kisses in doorways, no posies or ribbons. No tales about Orpheus. He paid court to Iskra, her sister instead. He laughed when Anelia knocked her headscarf askew, so that everyone laughed with him. And she began to believe the unthinkable: that he didn't care for her after all; that he had another lover, plaiting tokens for him somewhere in the village, that he would be singing his Christmas songs with thoughts for *her*. Nothing had been actually promised between them, after all.

And Anelia was not the only one to notice the change. Young Stefan, to whom Marko had always shown kindness before, suddenly felt himself discouraged, like a dog. Stefan was Aunt Kalina's youngest son, a block-headed boy who could manage no more than the simplest tasks and bore the brunt of the household's jokes and slanders. If something went missing, Stefan must have lost it. If the horse got out, Stefan must have forgotten the door. Stefan longed to be like Nikolai, respected and trusted. Nikolai would one day inherit the farm. He was his grandfather's favourite. Nikolai knew the sacred words that had to be said before the *budnik* was cut. Nikolai stood tall and straight as an oak himself. Stefan would never be loved so. He could only stand by and watch. When he was an old man, poor Stefan would still be sweeping straw and carrying water for the women. Now there was Marko too. Marko had stepped in amongst them like another son. Stephan had liked that at first. They were two outsiders together. But gradually Marko had begun to follow his own furrow. Moreover, Marko knew the world. He wasn't afraid to go up into the mountains alone. The respect in which Marko was held cast another shadow over Stefan.

And Stefan knew something else about him too. Marko had a gun.

When Nicolai set off to cut the Yule log that morning, Stefan slipped out of the house and followed him. The best oak trees grew in the forest beside the river and Stefan knew how to tread lightly and lie low like a fox. That was how he caught himself birds in the summer. Now he would steal some of Nicolai's magic. He would watch Nikolai and learn the sacred words he used. Then he would have something to console himself with with when Grandmother Hristova and the women scolded him.

Of course, he knew that what he was doing was wrong. He should have been feeding the chickens. Stealing magic, like saying the Mass backwards could open up pathways to damnation. But, for the moment, Stefan did not care. His bruised and jealous heart longed for validation and if Mary and the angels would not give it, well, he had no choice but to help himself. In any case, the rituals of Christmas Eve would protect him. He would carry his piece of garlic through the 'dirty days' to come and no devil could touch him as long as he kept that in his pocket.

He could not know that bad luck had already begun.

By midday, the *budnik* had been prepared, the festive breads were baked, but Stefan was nowhere to be seen. The men went out and called in case he had met with an accident. Aunt Kalina tutted and fussed, convinced he had drowned in the river. Old Grandfather Hristov knitted his brows.

"That boy will come to a bad end!" he growled. "Who is going to feed the pigs, eh? I suppose *I* am to take the swill out. He thinks he should be singing with the *koledari* this year. So he has taken himself off in a sulk. He is not sensible enough to do it. He does not know the songs. He should be here, where we can keep an eye on him. We must all stay together on this of all days. How shall we stop the sheep from straying and the hens from leaving their nests, if we cannot all sit down together for the Budni Vecher supper?"

But Stefan was nowhere to be found and the men returned empty handed. Marko arrived to hear the news.

Dusk fell.

They went through their holiday rituals with anxious hearts. After all, things *must* be done according to custom, perhaps even moreso, if there was trouble afoot. First, they lit the *budnik*. Grandfather brought coals and incense on a shovel and purified the room. And here came the loaf with the silver Lev buried somewhere inside it. Grandmother Hristova had fashioned the dough in a beautiful bas-relief, depicting sheep and beehives and milk-pails; symbols of prosperity on the farm. Here came the supper dishes, to be set side by side on the table, all eleven of them - an odd number - for even numbers were to be shunned on Christmas Eve. Beans there were and wheat and stuffed cabbage-leaves; all foods which swelled with cooking, to encourage the crops to swell next year. And down they all sat with everything to hand so that no one need rise till the end, for leaving the table would break the spell; the resin which would bind them together, safe and sure, for another year.

Even the dead had their place. Opposite Grandfather Hristov stood an empty chair, a welcome for the spirits of the departed. And when the feast was over, the dishes would be left all night on the *trapeza*, for the family ghosts to help themselves in case they were hungry and wanted to sit by the fire. But Stefan's vacant seat made a hideous symmetry. *Two* empty chairs. An even number. Grandfather Hristov made them push his stool away. He could not bear to look at it. It meant that Stefan could not now receive the blessings of Budni Vecher. Aunt Kalina cried into her sleeve.

105

And Iskra had tucked some ribbons into her hair. She sat smiling, her dark eyes dancing. Were they Marko's ribbons? Anelia did not doubt it. The lucky coin had turned up in Iskra's bread. Anelia had no stomach for her food. She saw her happy future slip away. She would not be a bride this year. She would not have a baby in her arms and take a posy to the midwife next Babinden. Her eyes welled with tears till the whole room swam. She hardly moved when the door burst open and someone staggered in. Well, *someone*! At first they were not sure if it was man or beast; a creature foaming at the mouth like a driven horse, eyes rolling, hair on end, but when he came into the lamplight they recognized Stefan.

"I've seen him!" he gasped, crashing to his knees. "*Karakondzuli*! I've seen the devil rider and his horse all covered in fire. I've seen him and his council sitting at their feast by the watermill! God save me, 'The Dirty Days' have come early and it is all my fault!"

Then he fell into convulsions and Kalina rushed to his side.

Uproar ensued. Nicolai's children set up a wail and tumbling from their stools, buried their faces in their mother's lap. Grandfather Hristov ordered everyone back to table. Stefan kicked up the straw rolling this way and that, then stretched himself out rigid and went blue.

That is it, thought Anelia. The end of us all. He has died a dreadful death and now he will come and haunt the house as a vampire. If it is true that the 'Dirty Days' have begun already, then he belongs to '*them*' and he will creep back at night and squeeze himself under the door as a bag of red blood to feast on our souls while we sleep. But whatever was he doing at the watermill? Didn't he know that ghouls and ghosts always haunt watery places? Did he *want* to see *karakondzhuli*? Had he already promised himself as a victim?

The family crept to their places and mumbled their way through their peas. Even Iskra kept her eyes downcast to hide the sparks of love that shone from them. Marko sat tight-lipped. Last of all came the nuts, the walnuts which Marko had brought. One by one they solemnly helped themselves, broke open the shells and, by the light of the kerosene lamp, inspected the kernels. This year they were good. Plump, firm, sweet. No blemishes, thank God! With every sigh, a little hope returned. Nikolai would have a good year, and mother and Grigor and even Aunt Kalina. Perhaps they could mend the misfortune Stefan had brought. Perhaps they could do things better at New Year, for another whole cycle of customs and festivals lay ahead; each season claiming its own saints, and special loaves and dances. Magic went on despite local tragedies - even despite the Turks.

Marko chose next and cracked himself a beauty and Anelia took hers with a trembling hand. Pray God, it would not matter, Stefan seeing the horseman. Pray God, he had already paid the price, drawn the evil on himself, away from her... Her walnut gave a rotten sound as it broke and out fell the wasted core, black as a crow-pecked lamb. With a cry she pushed it away.

Now she knew that she was truly damned.

At that instant there came a screech and a shuffle of feet outside which brought the meal to an end. The *koledari* were on their way. And here were the younger boys, running ahead, whooping, to warn that they were coming. The sound revived Stefan who gave a groan and Marko pounced upon him and dragged him to Grigor's bed where he called for water and wine and stroked his brow. "A dream, Stefan," he murmured, "You fell asleep in the wood. Forget it now. No harm is done."

In came the carol-singers, with their staves and their thick felt cloaks. A song for Grandfather Hristov and one for the sheep; one for the ploughshare; one for the apple trees. Good health! Long life! Then drinks all round and the women fetched their pretzels to hang on the singers' sticks. Blessings abounded and nobody thought any longer about *karakondzhuli*. They erased the memory, as though had never happened.

Marko and Grigor were to join the revellers and already they were getting into voice. Their tall fur hats, festooned with nuts and prunes, sported fresh-picked sprigs of evergreen box. Their cheeks glowed. Anelia had never seen Marko look so handsome. She hardly dared approach him. She felt so foolish now, with her elaborate love-bread. She wished she had hidden her heart in

107

something plain. But Marko hardly noticed the pretzel at all. Instead he gripped her fingers in his own and marched her to the porch.

"Anelia," he said, his white breath drifting out. "I have something to tell you."

"I know what it is," she replied.

"Do you?" He gave her a look, then fixed on the far horizon. "In a little while I shall be going away."

Now she turned to face him and her face was full of pain. "Are you? Are you taking her to the city then? Where your people came from?"

"*Her?*" He picked up the word as if it was a pebble and tossed it down again. "What *'her'?*"

"Iskra. I know you want to marry her."

"Oh, you silly goose! You poor, dumb, silly goose!" Marko brought his far-away gaze to meet hers and tightened his grip on her hand. "It is not about Iskra! I am yours. You *know* it already. Listen to me. This is about freedom."

Bewilderment took hold and Anelia tried to withdraw.

"Anelia," he hissed, marching her out into the dark. "The horseman Stefan saw. *I* have seen him too."

"I *knew* it! *I* have seen him."

"No, no. It is not what you think. This is no warrior-devil, no portent. Or rather, it *is* a portent. But of something wonderful and new. It is the biggest secret in the world but I know that you can keep it. Say you can keep it for me." He searched her face for something he could not find, then carried on, regardless. "The horse riders are *real*. They have come from Macedonia. They are rebels and they are going to help us fight the Turks. They fight them already, over there, behind the mountains. I have met them, spoken with them even. Some of our men are going to join them. *I* am going to join them. I am going to avenge my family. I cannot creep about here any longer, waiting for the next calamity. There's revolution coming and this time we are going to be free."

At last she understood.

"We are all going to die," she pronounced with calm solemnity. "Now the Yule log will go out, and we will never be happy again."

108

"Yule logs, cherry twigs, walnuts!" he smiled. "There are greater forces at work. Your walnut was *mine* in any case. *I* was the extra guest at supper and I took my nut before you. The rotten one was *mine*. So if anyone is to die, then I shall make sure that it is me, but it won't make any difference. I shall still be yours, whatever happens. I shall be with you when you feed the geese and when you knead your bread. I shall sit down to supper at your table and keep you warm in bed. No door will keep me out. Set me a chair next Christmas - I promise I will come!"

Anelia began to weep. "Then I shall be a widow before I am a bride and people will call me a witch because I have no children."

"All the children of Rhodope will be yours, because you let me go."

"What's that to me?"

"Something wonderful. Listen Anelia. Over to the East is a hill they call Perperikon. Peyo told me. Peyo is a poet, an educated man. On this hill are ancient tombs, walls older than you can imagine. Alexander the Greek consulted an oracle there and the Romans did the same. That oracle told fortunes, just like our *budnik*, but it was older than the Romans, older than the Greeks, and no one knows who heard it first. Curious, ancient things turn up in the soil. Coins and tiles and pots with pictures on them. Some of them show a horseman, just like ours, yours and mine and Stefan's. Do you know who he is? Not *Karakondzhuli*, the rider who must not be named. He is an older god, the hero-god of Thrace. You and I, we're Thracians, aren't we? Underneath these peasant clothes are the people of a great nation. This Thracian rider is killing a snake. And do you know who the snake is? It's Ottoman the Turk! We are going to rise up and surprise him. Next year, you'll see, even the Tsar of Bulgaria will give us his blessing and then there will be a proper battle and we will win this land back, just as they did at Stipka in the north. Then there will be no more wars, no more corruption and foreigners dictating what we do. Then we shall have dozens of children and dance the *horo* at all their weddings!"

She remained impassive. "What does it matter, who the snake is? Marko, death is death. He doesn't care."

Marko smiled. "Remember the old legends? Remember Orpheus? He travelled to darkest hell and back again. Well I shall do the same!"

"Marko, Orpheus died. They tore him to pieces and threw him in the river. You told me when you gave me the *silivriak* flowers. They are pink because they are stained with blood..."

Marko pushed her words aside. "Peyo says he is buried at Perperikon. Whoever can find his grave will bring him back to life. Then he will sing again and the prisoners of the underworld will rise up when they hear him."

Anelia shook her head. She was puzzling over something else: "Why the watermill? Why did the rebels meet *there*, on Christmas Eve? Everyone knows that old mills are haunted. And at Christmas the ghosts are everywhere."

"Precisely, you simpleton. It was a *secret* meeting. Where else can you light a fire without being seen? On Christmas Eve everyone is at home, preparing the family supper. And no one would go to a watermill on the eve of the 'dirty days' unless they wanted to make a pact with the devil! They could not imagine that that fool Stefan would be snooping about. Anelia you must take great care of him. Look after him. He must never know what he has seen. It is too dangerous."

The sound of voices rose behind them as the *kaledari* started to take their leave.

"Don't cry, my darling. Cheer up. Give me a kiss. Give me your blessing." He picked up the end of her plait and tickled her cheek. "You know how it is on Christmas Night. The gates of heaven open and if you are lucky you can see the angels. Can you see them?"

"I can see everything!" Anelia cried. "I have the gift you know. I have always seen things. I can see us scattered to the four winds. I see the wolf in the lamb pen. I see the black-throated cave which swallows the rivers of hell..."

"Careful, or you *will* be called a witch!"

"If I was a witch I could keep you."

"Here," he pulled a twig of winter cherry out of his hat and pressed it to her heart. "Keep this instead. This is the spirit of

110

Bulgaria. Now it is winter and the wood seems dead. But life is buried inside. Keep this somewhere warm and it will blossom, even if the snow is on the ground. This is like a song, waiting to be sung. It is my love for you. You cannot see it, but it will never die! And it is yours forever!"

He crushed her in his arms till her bones hurt and then turned to the carollers. They were setting off, laughing, pushing, juggling the lantern between them.

Anelia slipped away from the house, down to the riverside. Women must not come to the river in the 'dirty days'; they must not fetch water or spin, for the devil gets into water and...

What did it matter?

She crouched by the pebbles, listening to the river's song, and the stiff crackling of the bushes nearby.

"*Karakondzhuli!*" she called, softly. "*Karakondzhuli,* come out!"

The dark pressed itself upon her eyes, the shining dark of all her deepest fears. "*Karakonzhuli,* where are you?"

He would be able to find her easily enough. Her white embroidered sleeves hugged her knees; shining, drowned in the river's depths.

"Are you afraid, *Karakonzhuli?*"

The breathing dark pressed against her eyes.

"*Karakondzuli* are you listening? I will do a deal with you. I will give myself to you when I am dead, if only you will take back the bad luck. I will wash your shirts and bake your bread and feed your black geese, down in hell. But bring me Marko back alive."

Nothing stirred.

Only the river sang.

Over behind the mountain, a moon began to rise, flooding the upper sky. You could make out the dark crest of the ridge and the clouds that rode, like wild horsemen along it, mane and crest aflame with emerging light. Down here, the sinew of silver water snaked away. There were no ghosts to be seen.

Suddenly, Anelia jumped to her feet. Of course, there *was* a snake. But it was not the Turk. It was Death, pure and simple. Death took Eurydice. The horseman on the ancient coins was

111

Orpheus himself, battling to bring life back again. Just as baby Jesus did when he became a man. Life brought the *silivriak* flowers in spring. It brought the birdsong. It brought corn and hay out of the river. And it did not have a grave at Perperikon. It was everywhere, everywhere that a blade of grass could grow. And the songs were already *here*; the songs which the women sang, with their harsh, uncompromising voices. Their chants were like incantations from ancient times, from the hills and fields of Thrace, from the dark caves and the terrifying gorges of Rhodope itself. All the blood and all the conquests and the hopes of all the people in her land were in those songs. Chants which she could never sing because the fear of death had stolen her voice.

Well, perhaps she would stop being afraid. She watched the snake of the river under the moon.

Perhaps she would start to sing, herself, so that even if her world perished - the farm and the village and the rites of the Budni Vecher - there would still be song, flowing on like a river in people's minds. And freedom? Freedom was just *this* moment of believing in life and love. To love *this* moment and *this* life... She turned back towards the farmhouse lights...

She would put her twigs in water and see what they would do.

Grimalkin

Reader's Note

The literary references in this tale allude to the world of fact, though they rub shoulders with fiction. Whereas William Baldwin is known to have lived and died, Jug and his master, Bullinger, are phantoms of the imagination, as are all who believe in them. Their haunted house in Hertfordshire, mere make-believe...

But the Grimalkin... the Grimalkin, is something else. Neither living nor dead, this creature certainly exists and you cannot go far amongst the ways of men, without noticing the demon print of its paws...

Grimalkin

As to the question of talking cats, the matter has never been satisfactorily resolved. William Baldwin presents us with a Grimalkin in his novel of 1553. The 'Furred Law-Cats' of Rabelais, a decade later, have a deal to say. And we are familiar with the Tabithas and Brindles of children's fables. But the reality of a cat which concerns itself with human affairs... which plays with human destiny, as any hob-cat might play with a mouse... well, that is altogether a more troublesome concept and one which returns to puzzle those with curious minds.

Edward Bullinger was one such. He was born in Edmonton, a few steps from the cottage which Charles and Mary Lamb made their last home. And it has been suggested that poor Mary, with her history of insanity, haunted his youthful imagination. Certainly, he nursed a graveyard temperament from an early age. Ruskin and the British Museum may have shaken the cobwebs from the ancient world, bringing it before the public in a new and rational light. But Bullinger's heart remained a refuge for shadows in exile. As a boy, he had read Shakespeare - a corrupted text - which included the Edmonton play, once ascribed to him. And he quickly perceived how fact and fiction wound themselves together, like the cat and the proverbial table leg.

Whoever its rightful author, in 1608 *'The Merry Devil of Edmonton'* amused the king, and thirteen years later, the good folk of that place arraigned their own witch who was duly hanged at Tyburn. Straightaway, Dekker and friends set to work to put the trial on stage and *'The Witch of Edmonton'* went down well with the groundlings.

No one, thereafter, could tell for sure the proper facts of the case: whether the woman was wronged or no; a foolish mischief-maker or a poor old wretch with one eye and a wart, as seemed the common view. We, who enjoy the luxury of being humane, see horror on every side. But then, a modern judge can hardly guess what fears lurked then in people's minds - fears which plainly flourished amidst the manifold ills of the day. And would we do better in their place?

Magic must have seemed both friend and foe. For crosses and hidden shoes; rowan trees planted at the door and elder twigs in cowsheds; they might help a little to keep the falling sickness, or the blight at bay. But were such things sufficient? Prayers were all very well in church, but who knew what was muttered backwards in the dark of the graveyard after? How to protect the child in the cradle? The milk in the dairy? How to keep out the curses of vermin and plague? How plug the back-door draughts which let death in? The Halloween faces of the lame and old showed mortality at work. They were weak spots where life peeped into the void. Drive them out. Pelt them out. Like pelting a cat in a pot. Bundle up all the pain and punish it. That would be the way! And who, granted the thrill of heaving with a mob, would be proof against tempting, once their fears were roused?

Bullinger loved the theatre, though his own particular bent was musical. Yet, though the Victorians lapped up grisly tales, somehow, he never managed to make his mark. Opera was the love-child of the English stage. Buffeted between the Music Halls, blood tubs and the high drama of Irving and Keane, few homespun works outlived their opening run and those that did were of the sentimental kind. While the Italians and Germans seized the chance to make their operas 'grand', the English showed a preference for comedy and romancing the past in pantomime tights. Bullinger could not be content with ballads. His ambition stirred to darker motifs. So when the Chetham Society reprinted '*Beware the Cat*', he secured himself a copy; soaked up the tone of 1553 - Bloody Mary just ascending the throne - and secretly sharpened his quills. He would rework the '*Witch*' in a form which would send his European rivals packing.

'*Elspeth Farley*', the opera which ensued, was to dominate a life's descent into madness. How he wrestled with his score! Butchered it, pasted it, sweated nights over it. He needed no magic to open his ears. An addiction to Dover's Powder, - opium, to alleviate headaches - proved ample stimulus and it was soon a small matter for him to forget his friends. In all honesty, he alarmed them. He showed a marked intolerance towards mankind, taking comfort, instead, in the company of his cat, a great striped beast called 'Jug'.

By now he had moved from London, taken up residence in Hertfordshire and begun a dubious affair with his housekeeper; a woman who claimed that she could talk with the dead. His cat went too.

Had his master lived a more successful life, Jug might have attained celebrity himself, like Dr. Johnson's Hodge, and Lear's stupendous Fosse. Jug had all the requisites. Torn ears. Yellow eyes. Fat paws. A bald nose, raked with scars. Jug undoubtedly inspired the familiar which played cat's-paw to Bullinger's crone. In the new libretto, Jug replaced Dekker's demon 'dog' and secured an aria all to himself. And by this masterstroke – (inspired by the chorus which had tormented rooftop London since the days when cats were scaffold scavengers) - he was able to reveal that the 'witch' was a pawn of Fate. But that evil *had* walked abroad. And guess how it was done?

To his concerned contemporaries, the tragedy which followed seemed all but inevitable. One night, when opiates had clouded both eyes and brain, Bullinger, having stuffed his ears with wool, stabbed his poor servant as she was laying the fire and spent his remaining days in an asylum. His papers passed to a pupil of MacFarren. 'Hallways', his Hertfordshire home, fell into ruin. No further mention appears to be made of Jug.

Matters stood thus until 1895, when Bullinger died and Albert Knowles the spiritualist, 'took him over'. Now Knowles had money and friends and influence and, as is well-known, never missed an opening when he saw one. To rescue Bullinger from obscurity would, at one stroke, give English opera the weight it needed and provide a perfect subject for research. What better way to promote his psychomantic dreams?

His plan of action was clear. First secure the house. Then find the man who could impose some order on the score. '*Elspeth Farley*' would be brought before the public. And the truth, the truth which had driven England's finest composer out of his wits, would be revealed.

No less an architect than Fiddes was employed to restore 'Hallways'. The finest red brick and English oak furnished the property with an Arts and Crafts elegance and poise. Simplicity, sturdiness, integrity. Comfort for guests. A library for research. William Morris on the walls and delphiniums in the gardens. Knowles himself moved in and held Bullinger weekends for devotees who paid. The ghost of Bullinger promptly beat a retreat, though an opera of sorts was staged.

Critics, however, could never agree about '*Elspeth*'.

The monumental fragments had been stitched together with homely thread, a kind of musical placeholder, or 'lorem ipsum' which left an uneasy sense of what was lost. It was a Stone Henge of an opera - more gaps than stones - like Manet's '*Maximilian*' painting, whose severed parts, once rescued by Degas, were brutally patched with squares of unprimed canvas. Yet the sequence of the parts, so critical to any grasp of their intent, remained a matter of speculation. How should the opera end? With Jug? With Elspeth? With the townsfolk who tormented her? With Master Pipe, the judge, who condemned her to torture and death? To make matters worse, Jug's aria could not be found. According to Knowles' medium, the music had gone up the chimney. So that was the end of that, or so it was thought. And another whole century passed before a postscript could be added.

Knowles had long been discredited as a charlatan who battened on his followers' credulity. Disappointed in his own professional hopes, he was known to have stage-managed the ghosts and spirit-writings for which his time at Hallways was famous. Collaborating with a local photographer, he himself posed for the series of ectoplasmic studies depicting a figure in the garden - a figure naturally identified by his beard and stocky build, Victorian cape and bowler - as the unfortunate Bullinger. He had employed all the tricks of the dark room for his effects, using double-exposures and tampering with the negatives, to the extent of painting in the figure of the cat. He might have got away with it, too, had he not lost his nerve and made a full confession.

The chicanery was regrettable, but Knowles' admissions brought the whole spiritualist community into disrepute. A hail of abuse and ridicule ensued. The Archbishop of Canterbury made a statement. And, as many thought, the matter ended ignominiously, with Knowles, a shadow of his former self, being received into the Church of Rome and taking refuge in a Belgian pension. That, mark you, not before he had developed a pathological fear of cats and tried on several occasions to set fire to the house. Thereafter, his executors discreetly removed any reminder of Edward Bullinger and sold the property to an American buyer.

In 1995, the centenary of Bullinger's death, 'Hallways' came onto the market once again. And this time it was bought by public subscription. Everyone wanted a museum. A Bullinger Trust was formed and volunteers scoured the country hoping to find at auction the effects which had been lost. Lo and behold! Remnants of the composer's furniture, old letters, old gloves and walking-sticks, salvaged from oblivion, soon came winging back to their original home. A curator was appointed. Someone donated an inkwell. Someone else returned a key. The original wallpaper was uncovered. They located the site of the well. Wrote a guide book. Built a ticket office... And booked a date for an official opening. All that remained was to order champagne, invite the press and light a fire in the study. December 23rd was the chosen date. I myself was invited to it. As Bullinger's biographer, I would naturally play my part. And my musicologist friend, Professor. Hurdey, respected Chairman of the Board of Trustees, had promised to come from Cambridge to give an address. Imagine my surprise, therefore, when, he phoned at breakfast time and I knew from the tone of his voice that something was up:

"Maurice, they've *got* it. I do believe they've got the thing at last."

"Got what, you fool?" I replied, with that bantering disrespect we always reserved for one another.

"Shut up and listen. No joking now. I'm driving over to Hoxton and I'll pick you up on the way. Some idiot at 'Hallways' has brought down half the chimney. Virtually destroyed the place. There is no way the opening can go ahead, as planned. But you won't believe it - they have found some papers. Heaven knows how old. Papers hidden in the brickwork. And the oddest thing..." (Here, I confess, my flesh began to creep.) "...as if it was an ancient house - which of course it *isn't* - they found a mummified cat. This is *it* - do you understand? We have struck our gold!"

'Hallways' stood in a wood bordering the high, flinty fields just south of Hitchin. I had been there many times before, envying the cosy atmosphere of the villages en route: toy cottages with liquorice beams and dormer casements peeping from under the thatch. Stately, grey churches. Streams and ponds. There seemed to be a perpetual breeze sighing over the land, which raised a chorus in the wood itself. Some said it was a morbid place, but it had never seemed so to me. I loved the feel of the solid gates, the latches, locks and shutters, all secure. When a moon sailed overhead, it looked a piece of poetry. In this winter light, the roof retained a rime of frost. I could not imagine any part of it falling down.

The young curator met us in the drive.

"Thank God you've come! Someone needs to talk to the press. I've e-mailed everyone I can, but my computer, all my files are *in there*. The accident has put out the electrics, which can be fixed, but first we need to stabilise the site. No one can enter till the architect says it is safe and he is in Adelaide visiting his daughter for Christmas. I feel so horribly responsible. We had the chimneys swept some weeks ago but the fire in the study simply wouldn't draw. Smoke everywhere, each time we tried to light it. And of course we had planned to hold the Trustees' party there. I managed to book a new sweep yesterday. And now, when everything is ready to go - well, the whole thing is a disaster." She stood on tiptoe, nervously twisting her hair.

Hurdey took charge.

"Cancel the opening. Say there has been an accident. Unavoidable delay. Time needed for the conservators to make an assessment... We can turn this situation to our advantage. The right headlines will boost publicity... The timing couldn't have been better, really: '*Bullinger returns to solve final mystery...*' We've booked ourselves in at The Forester's Arms. Anything we can do to help..."

She winced a smile. "The other Trustees are on their way. You want to see the damage?" That went without saying. "It's this way, round at the back. I'm worried about security. Anyone might get in. Somebody vandalised the Christmas tree at Elmley only two days ago. We don't expect that kind of thing round here."

"Not to worry," breezed Hurdey. "We'll camp out if necessary. You've got the papers safe?"

"Peter Hanson picked them up. The burglar alarm went off when the wall fell down and that rang through to his private house. He's the caretaker. He found the devastation when he arrived. Of course he shouldn't have gone in but he wasn't to know. The cat was poking out of the wall. Gave him a fright, I think. The advisor from English Heritage said touch nothing, but we couldn't leave things as they were. Suppose it rained. Suppose a fire broke out. We moved what we could to the library and locked it all away. We may have missed one or two items but the police won't let us anywhere near again."

Hurdey winked. "Lead the way!" he said. And we trooped round into the garden.

Bullinger's study stood on the ground floor, facing west. It would, in any case, have been hard to picture the room as he had known it, Fiddes having done so much to change it. Now altered

121

beyond recognition, it looked as though a bomb had whistled through. A hole gaped where the chimney had tumbled down. Debris lay scattered on the lawn. Wisps of tape on construction spikes now marked the area off.

"It's going to cost thousands. Hundreds of thousands to repair. The caterers will have to be paid... It couldn't have happened at a more difficult time." The curator's litany of woes, dribbled on, like the leak from a faulty tap.

"No help for it!"

"My fiancé was taking me to Bath..."

"And *no* reason to cancel that. We'll speak to Mr. Hanson - organize the press. You borrow a computer and pacify the punters. You can use our rooms at the hotel down the road. We'll set up head-quarters there. Find a builder. Find that chimney-sweep! And I want to speak to the local Chief Constable. The rest can be dealt with after Christmas."

I have to say he was magnificent. And all the time he kept a tight reign on his thoughts, which showed themselves only as a gleam in his eye.

What a day that was! My head spun in a whirl. Hurdey chivvied, commiserated and dictated as occasion demanded. With the press he was suave, with the law he was grave. His natural bonhomie soothed anxieties. His energy inspired hope. The Trustees gratefully handed their responsibilities to him. They too had families, parties, last minute shopping to attend to. The builder promised scaffolding by dusk. Even Hanson, who had retreated behind a wall of defensive excuses, dropped his surliness and finally began to talk. A bottle of scotch proved useful in bringing him out...

"The sweep had arrived at four," he said. "Cocky sort. Claimed there was nothing he didn't know about chimbleys. He checked them all over and then he come to the study. Had a cup of tea. Rolled back the carpet and rigged up his cloths. He liked to do it the old way, he said, through a hole in a sheet. Keep all the soot in the hearth. Chatting all the time, he was, about the village. How his folk had been sweeping chimbleys hereabouts for hundreds of years. He's feeding the rods through one after another, screwing

122

them on and working them further up, when suddenly he hits an obstacle. Birds' nest, is it? Tar? Whatever it is, he can't budge the thing for love nor money. But the chimbley's *got* to be cleared. They've booked the school children to sing carols for the opening - mince pies - mulled wine. Local television's coming. They need a fire in the study, to look Christmassy, even though the underwriters moan.

"'Funny thing about this chimbley,' says the sweep. 'It's older than the house.'

"'How do you reckon that then?'" (Hanson did the different voices, pinching his nose with his thumb.)

"'I know a lot about this house,' he says. 'Like I know the chimbley belongs to another cottage that was on this site before.'

"'Never!'

"'And, what's more, that cottage had a witch in it and it was one of my ancestors as set fire to it. You look on an old map. You won't find no 'Hallways' here. The cottage that stood on this spot in the 1700s was called 'All Hallows'. And a witch lived in it, sure as I'm alive today. The mischief she done has all been forgotten now, but folk were more knowing then. They went to her for herbs, herbs and charms, and some of those herbs spirited the life out of them. Cattle went dry. Rot got in the wheat. It never stopped raining. And the bonniest children fell sick and died. One night they took the law into their own hands, came with torches and set alight to the thatch. Mother Broomstick flew out of the chimbley and vanished on a trail of smoke. And they all went home to their beds and never breathed a word about it. Just the chimbley, which was stone, was left. Years after, the place was rebuilt and passed to a gentleman from London. It would be his grandson as sold it on to Bullinger."

"'But did Bullinger know all this?' says I

Hanson heaved a shrug.

"'How could he?' says the sweep. 'I've got a tool to clear that blockage with' and out he goes and fetches a prod from his van. I didn't know he was going to bring the whole bloody building down."

"So nothing happened then," prompted Hurdey.

"He dislodged some bricks. The rest must have shifted later, after we'd gone home. I reckon the beam had rotted. You couldn't see it from this side. If you ask me, that architect's to blame - couldn't tell a plumb-line from a plum pudding. He should have known if the chimbley was old and rotten... "

"More whisky!"

"Ta!"

"But the documents. How old were they? Why were they in the chimney, Peter?"

"They done that kind of thing for good luck, didn't they, years gone by? Shoes and that. Children's shoes. They used to wall them up. I saw it on the telly. Cats were a favourite, too. 'Sposed to keep the Evil One away."

"Four hundred years ago perhaps. Are these that old?"

"Not to my way of thinking. The writing's on paper. Tied up in envelopes. They never had envelopes then, did they?"

"And the cat?"

Hanson shrugged again. "Still got its fur. I'm not an expert on cats."

"What about the sweep? Has anyone spoken to him?"

"Cowboy! Not a trace of him anywhere. Maybe he's done a runner. Phone number's unobtainable. His e-mail doesn't exist."

"Curioser and curioser!"

"You're enjoying it, aren't you? But all this has probably cost me my job." Hanson sniffed into his glass.

"*I* think you may have done something tremendous! I think you may have found what we've been searching for, for years. One missing aria. One missing cat. What was it Bullinger said? Gone up the chimney... Now we shall learn the truth."

The long day finally came to a close. We dismissed the staff, for their well-earned Christmas break, retired to the Forester's Lodge and ate some supper. Our plan was to stay there overnight and return to tie up loose ends the following morning. Dr. Norris from the British Library was due at ten. Eschewing dessert, we decamped to finish the Scotch. Our mood had swung throughout the day, from exhaustion to elation, frustration and despair. Whisky induced a state of recklessness. We might have been schoolboys plotting some term-time prank. A tuck-shop raid - a rooftop dare - we'd done such things before when we were young.

"I'll tell you what we'll do," said Hurdey, seizing me by the arm. "We'll borrow a torch and we'll go and take a look. I've got the key. That Mildew girl gave it to me."

"Mildew?"

"Cardew. Whatever. We'll go and look for ourselves."

"Don't be crass, you ass. Every burglar alarm in the county will go off."

"Not *there*. I know the code. I know everything. I know the combination of the key safe. I even know where they've put the mince pies and candles! Come on. Don't say you're not up to it! We'll just *look* - see if the aria's there before the British Library confiscate it for months. It's the chance of a lifetime. And if I'm right... well then, *we'll* have the answer, won't we? We'll be the *only* people in the world who do?"

"We'll be the only people to spend our Christmas, buried under a pile of rubble."

"Not if that builder chappie has done his job. Oh, for heaven's sake. Where's your sense of adventure? Get your coat. This is better than Christmas, Matt. This is fame on a plate. Oh Jug, Jug..." With that he burst into song *"Ha, ha, he – he, he, he , Little brown Jug don't I love thee!"*

Somehow we stumbled out into the night, past the village lights and down into the wood. We pushed and jogged one another, tripped and cursed - sang ourselves snatches of Gilbert and Sullivan. At the entrance we opened the gate, and crept along the drive. Here, on the right, stood the ticket office and shop. Further on, the dark mass of the house itself. An owl called out over the wood. Much fumbling with torch and key and in we went.

No problem with the alarm. The library lay straight ahead. But at this point, I have to confess, my courage failed me. I was overcome by a sudden sense of loathing. My knees melted. My tongue felt like an old shoe in my mouth. I did not want to meet Jug face to face. I did not want to learn how he had met his fate. I did not want to know what he had to tell us. The accumulated foulness of all the deeds in the house suddenly pressed upon me, but Hurdey brushed them aside.

"The beast is dead isn't it? The whole world is going to see it when the press get in."

In point of fact, Jug did not seem to be there. Miss Cardew must have put him somewhere else. We found the bundle of papers right enough, retrieved them from their glass-topped cabinet, spread them on the desk and lit some candles. There was no mistaking - here was Bullinger's hand. Close scribbling, sheet after sheet, in his heavy script but no musical notation. No music at all. Where was the aria? We took a page a-piece and, between mouthfuls of cake, we scanned the text for clues. The whisky kept us steady. We had raided the room where the party food was stacked and filched some stollen and a knife to cut it. Cosy it was, by the flickering candle-light and a wind got up and spat rain at the windows. Somewhere out in the wood, a cat yowled and broke off.

Hurdey laughed at that. "Gone out for a walk, has he?" he joked, brushing his crumbs aside.

They were diary entries mostly. Records of conversations with Mrs. G. - that fateful year of 1872:

'March 22nd. Mrs. G. Tells me that she is 'psytic' - that is her term - She has known 'them' ever since she was a girl. Not that it bothers her. She is nothing if not pragmatic. This house is full of 'them' she says. Unquiet...'

'Sept 4th. More talk with Mrs. G. She can't abide the cat. I told her plainly - Jug's the master here. He won't tolerate being left out in the cold. Frost early. Worked till 2. Then walked and worked late. Fire went out. Always going out in this wretched room.'

*'Dec 12th. Premonitions. Bad dreams again. Mrs. G. puts it down to eating pork. I told her that that was nonsense and she insisted. When she was younger, she says, she always **knew** when someone was going to die. The same premonition on numerous occasions. A door opening, to her inward view, and a figure passing through. Then the door closing. Never got it wrong. She was a poor sleeper. Stomach very bad. Tried everything. Kendal Black Drop. Collis Browne's. It wasn't till she gave up pork that she could experience any relief. But then the power of premonition*

vanished too. Now she only hears... I told her to write it down. Anything which might help... But she won't tell. Not yet.'

'Dec 15th. She has decided to talk at last. My God! Now I understand about the chimney - but Jug... Jug is the key. Soon I can finish things...'

"There must be more," cried Hurdey, holding up his page. "There must be more than this. There must be a record somewhere of what she said. What *Jug* said, dammit. If he finished the opera, where did he hide the score?"

"Perhaps he was too far gone to get it down. Perhaps he burnt it" said I.

Hurdey dismissed this out of hand.

"No. He had ten whole days before he finally snapped." He staggered to his feet. "There must be other papers somewhere here - hidden in the rubble. I'm going to look."

"You're drunk!"

"I'm going to be five minutes. I'll get some more food as well. You can wait here if you're afraid to come."

With that he grabbed the torch and lurched to the door. "Five minutes!" he shouted as he passed through. And the draught promptly snuffed my candles out.

Somehow I panicked - lost the will to move. Sat in the dark with the wind spitting rain at the windows, thinking how lonely it must have been, surrounded all night by those ever-whispering trees. How one might lie here, fearful of shapes in the dark and no one to hear if a body cried out for help. Worse. If lights and voices meant evil coming... A torch for the thatch... Who would not reach for magic, if magic was all the protection you could have? Who would not curse the cow of a man who put your cat in the well? The law? The law was not made for lonely folk. The law itself danced a pretty line between fear of the mob and deference to the rich. And what judge, faced with riots, with priests, with nervous men at court - rick-burnings, lynchings, preference and superstition would not take the line of least resistance - bundle his fears into a palpable shape and hang that shape, with a prayer, from the nearest gibbet?

Reason could reach thus far. But then, the cat? The cat was where my reason came unstuck. Jug, the Grimalkin, purring by the fire - crouching in the hallway - hissing on the stairs. What message from the devil did he bring? Mrs. G had heard it - remember, she couldn't abide the cat. And when she told it to Bullinger it drove him out of his wits. God knows how terrible the struggle must have been between Jug and his master. Knowles heard it too, from that so-called medium of his. Why else his sudden flight amongst the nuns? And the business was not finished yet. The score - I did not believe there was a score for words which could unhinge the human brain - but someone without question would be next... some unsuspecting fool would succumb and the evil would go on. Bullinger had stuffed his ears, trying to keep the poison out... But the wind cannot be stilled by wishing. Anything may travel on the wind - seek out the vibrant ossicles, panicles, fibrillae, which stimulate the mind. Worse. Suppose the words came from within? Spontaneously summoned, without recourse to books - to spells - to febrile incantations... Baldwin's patent brew...

No mopping or mowing,
No mewing or crowing,
No crying or wauling,
Wailing or squalling,
Squealing or crabbing,
Cribbing and blabbing
Blubbing and ...

Once shut in the dark, the mind could conjure with ease any shape to carry its desires. It were the easiest thing in the world to see Jug now, a shadow amongst the shadows on the lawn - a slip of a shadow, sidling along the hall - licking his paws - waiting, poised to pounce...

My thoughts were arrested by a padding sound and the thump of something soft outside the door. A muffled, scrabbling, followed. Claws on wood.

"Hurdey?" I called out, half-congealed with fright. "Hurdey, don't be an idiot. It isn't funny, you know."

Silence drummed and then came the reply - a high-pitched, whining, mewling, tom-cat waul. My heart broke into a canter.

Cold sweat came. The sound of my voice appalled me when I heard it:

"Hurdey?" Hurdey was dead. Had I not seen him only moments before, pass into darkness through that very door? And had I not just heard the cat confirm it? Jug was there, palpably there dictating to my mind. And mind? My mind now flooded with a terrible light. Yes! It was clear to me now. Dark deeds were not the evil, after all, but symptoms merely - albeit vile enough - of something we all *knew*, kept like a hearth cat in our homes, not guessing the harm it could do. The evil itself was fear. Fear, which had torn my reason out of me. Already too late...

By the time Max set his foot inside the door, juggling a cheese and a plate of vol-au-vents, a baguette firmly gripped between his teeth, I had already hurled the knife which finished him...

Knockings

Knockings

A night like pitch and the wind blowing savage and me all alone in this cold, dark house! A night like this, when Joseph Samson drowned in his own well and that great beech broke down the gable end of The Saracen's Head. Nothing to be heard, but the rain pattering, hard and nagging, like a birch brand, scolding the windows and the wind in the rowans and the beck raging.

The nights I've spent in the open, gipsying: Father cursing and pushing the shafts with his shoulder, while the cart strained backwards down Hindfoot Lip and me running about in the rain looking for rocks to wedge behind the wheels - and Mother with Nolly and Will, no more nor little babes, huddled, tired in the back. Good days! I never felt the cold then and always, in the evening, there was some lamp-lit inn and a bed for us and the big men tweaking my hair and laughing. Me, scarcely as tall as the table. God be thanked, the bright memories last longest! I could see us now, sitting on the tailboard of the wagon, a hunk of bread a-piece, sitting in the sunshine, while the old horse drank from the river, kicking up a splash to cool her sides. Father and Mother had been shouting about drinking money and he picked up his hat and stalked away with those great, long strides of his and she cried into her shawl a good half-hour after. At last, she sits up straight and says it's the chance of her life - she's as good a carrier as he, any day of the year And she jumps down and untethers the horse and begins to curse no end. I wouldn't help, wanting my Daddy back, so she harnessed Jessie alone, till I was proud of her being so strong and reckless. It was a great adventure, us setting off alone and all the hillsides green and mauve with heather and the river singing beside us. We'd twelve miles to go, I remember, along the bonniest patch of road, with bits of woodland and lush grass and the rowans all crusty with lichen and the berries reddening. We started off singing too and then fell silent and then we'd cry a bit and then mother would toss her head and start another song. And, thinking of how we'd been together in the morning, we'd cry again...

A shutter banging? The wind'll get into the strongest of houses. I remember how the door blew open at Whiteside. The wind knocked, all by itself and came right in... Now, where am I? Lost my thread and my eyesight is bad for joining on again.

The wind, the wind - steady. ...the night Joseph Samson was drowned at Fellbarrow... lost it again. Well, here I am now in the empty house and my aunt is a devil of a long time coming back... Oh, yes. The knocking, the knocking that frightened the wits from me the night Jill Dawkins died of twins.

Aunt Hesther, she was called out in the filthy dark, to see to the other children. Six of them there were and Mr. Dawkins wouldn't leave the corpse. And I begged and I begged her to take me and she wouldn't, but built up a warm fire, cosy and checked the shutters and gave me oatcake and a pile of wool and said very stern I wasn't to set a foot out of doors, but to have the yarn spun by the time she got back. And it was a big wheel, hers was, taller than me when I sat to it. One of those with the maiden to the side and a squeaking axle that seemed like company. It was wool, not flax and I was glad of that, but I kept thinking of the six children in the valley and of the hungry babies and the woman laid out and them combing her hair and spreading new sheets on the bed... And then I heard a knocking in the closet room above and I froze like a tree, with my arms up, checking the wheel. And I thought of Moll Dawkins ghost, in her long, white shift, with her tresses hanging down and no shoes on her feet. I thought of her stealing across the boards upstairs and rattling the door-latch. She's come to fetch me because my own mother died - because I cheated little Sally over the seed-cake. I can hear every sound in the valley. I can hear the clouds moving and the smoke drifting out through the birch boughs, and the lights burning in the end cottage...

She was nice-looking - gipsy-looking and tall, not like my mother. Mine was a rough skirt and rosy face - and then Aunt Hesther was thin, but she was old... The knocking came again. Lordy me! She's on the stairs. And me? I dropped my yarn and fled to the door and out away down the steps to the high road. And

I ran all the way to Moll Dawkin's house and never looked back and I never had such a scolding in my life...

But that's how I've been always - timid in my mind - and always things have turned out fair enough. The day my parents quarrelled I thought we'd never see my father again - and lo, when we got to the Swan at dusk, there he was to meet us at the coach house, arms crossed and a beaming smile on his face. He'd seen the cart travelling on from the high fell, where his temper had taken him, and then continued at a pace behind us, out-stalked us and ordered hot potatoes for supper. These days, men aren't of that kind. Losing them young, I remember my people better - the good *old* sort I loved. My brothers were well enough, but they got an education and it weakened them somehow. They were all thinking and no talking, or all talking and no doing. They couldn't have been carters after that.

Now where am I? Wool-gathering, always wool-gathering. Many's the beating I got from my Aunt Hesther, for dreaming. And I couldn't a-bear it.

So, you see, Jack Pointy, though I didn't like your face, it's why I said I'd have you. Shepherding's nothing to carting. What is there for a shepherd's wife to do, but gossip at the well and toil in a draughty house? Fine days, when the sun's on the heaf and the curlews are calling, when the lambs race at dusk, *you're* on the fell with the green fern. Winter time, you're numbed blue and sodden, but you see the snowy tops and you've company in your sheep. Me? I'm in the house-place, dark still, with the stench of peat and a cradle to rock! Oh I'd rather have had the highroad any day. Where's the housework when you're only home to sleep?

I've sat here nights enough, with a child on my knee, spinning the hours away, while you were spinning other yarns at The Black Horse. God love you, you could always tell a good story. No man like Jack Pointy for grimacing, or lying! And I was proud enough of that. But times when I've waited alone, thinking you'd fallen in a ditch, or a mire; times when you went to look for sheep and came home at midnight, singing... I didn't love you then, Jack, and I'll wager you felt it. I'd sit here, treddling my thoughts into a rage and I liked it to be windy then and hear the boughs rap on the windows.

And sudden I'd think of one of your tales - of a song you'd sing and I'd see you, coughing in your chair by the fire and the ghost of you would make me weep. I see you now lean forward with your cold, blue eyes and your hair all over your head and you lift up your finger with a smile none could ever resist: "I'll tell you a story - a *true* story, mind..."

Like the true story of Hesther's ghost. *That* was a broom falling down the outside stairs. And who put it there? I did myself! But it didn't spoil the story a bit of it, or save the chill racing down my spine.

Twist and feed, twist and feed - the wheel comes round full circle. I've sat in the room when I was sick, longing for a sound that might be someone coming. All silent, and a clear moonshine, still I put a lamp in the porch to welcome even the beggars that might call. And I've outlived them all and I'm afraid of none of them now. I'm no longer keen to be out on the road, but happy with this house.

There - broke my thread again and I'll fasten that shutter while I'm up on my feet. It's banging like someone stepping on the stairs - and - Lord have mercy, the door'll come open, shaking so, with such a bright light beyond...

Enter a stranger

Stranger: Who are you and what's your business?

Ghost: I'm a free body in my own home

Stranger: *Your* house, is it?

Ghost: Ay, and has been since I could call a house my own.

Stranger: Then you've trespassed a long while. This house is my mind and all its contents are nothing but dreams and fables and ghosts. You startled the wits out of me with your knocking and mumbling there.

Ghost: Startled you? *You*? And here's me quaking with fear. If it's your house, come in and welcome. Don't dither by the door. Come and take a seat, only, don't turn me out just yet. It's a rough night and lonely and I only want a little longer to finish my task. Don't cut me off before I've done. I'm an old woman, after all...

Stranger: Tell me, quick then, where did you come from?

136

Ghost: Who knows? Who knows?

Stranger: And what are you doing?

Ghost: Plying threads to weave you a story for your own old age...

Dooley's Bar

Dooley's Bar

Every Christmas, we would go carol singing at Dooley's Bar. Dooley was a big, loose-limbed Irishman with an open, affable manner and a mop of curly, brown hair, which he ruffled a good deal in the course of his conversation. He had been a chorister, when a boy, at the Trinity Chapel in Dublin and so remarkable was the purity of his top C, and the sweetness of his devotion, there had been talk of him going to the Vatican. However, delays of one sort or another in the labyrinths of church bureaucracy, and a certain churlishness on the part of the local cardinal, who was loath to lose him, ruined his chances, and when his voice finally broke it descended into his boots.

Undeterred, Dooley turned his energies to other pursuits. He also had talent, time revealed, in the spheres of drinking and gambling, and since he was always willing to buy the next round with his winnings, no one begrudged him success. Dooley could not resist taking a risk. He graduated from student bars to the stock exchange, and when his investments crumbled, took to the property market. At thirty-four he owned a string of properties in Mayfair, including the building just off Leicester Square. And it was here, every year, that he indulged his childhood love of music, with an informal sing-along which lasted well into the early hours.

Those of us who were regulars in the West End, found an invariable welcome at Dooley's. Clientele was by personal recommendation, for there was hardly any indication in the street below, of the snug comforts and heart-warming food to be had within. Those who 'knew', turned in at the side stairs and mounted to the first floor where the smell of sausage and colcannon awaited them. Pies! You never saw such pies as Dooley served. Bacon pot. Beef pudding... And the blackest Guinness and melting, golden whiskey... and after closing, while the chefs were cleaning the kitchen, and Dooley's son slept at his table with his little blond head on his arms, out would come the cards and to the tune of the most companionable conversation in the world, we would fritter our money away as if it was a privilege and a pleasure to empty our pockets.

During the weeks before Christmas, Dooley got into voice. Christmas lights festooned every inch of the Bar. A nativity scene worthy of a cathedral, with hand-carved figures from Harrods, occupied the window bay. There were candles galore. We half expected to find censors swinging from the ceiling, but we took it all with a wink, thinking this was Dooley's way of showing the Pope he could match Vatican any day, or perhaps it was laid on for the boy, since his Christmas, sitting on a hard chair alone, while the men played poker, would be a bleak one.

Young Donald was a queer little fish; a pale-faced, silent child. Customers would pat him on the head, or fling him a couple of quid, feeling embarrassed by his presence. The head chef would send him out special bowls of chips, while he did his homework. It all seemed to be the same to him. And in the end it was easier to ignore him, as his father did, and get on with the business of enjoying ourselves. No one ever asked why the boy was not at home with his mother. No one ever asked if he even had a mother. Behind the smile and the tousled hair, Dooley harboured an impenetrable reticence that prohibited enquiry.

"Take life as you find it!" said the motto above the Bar. That was good enough for us.

The first year that Dooley advertised the carols, some singers turned up from Covent Garden and rose to the challenge of out-singing the traffic below. Dooley opened the windows and stationed his waiters, with buckets, in the street, collecting donations from passers-by. Standing there, in the draughty candlelight, with the glitter of Christmas all around us, we sang out together as if our lives depended on it and drew such a crowd that the police had to usher people on. The highlight came with 'Once in Royal' and Dooley doing a very passable falsetto for the treble solo. The collection buckets filled to overflowing and we all downed considerable quantities of Christmas punch and laughed very much at our own jokes till it was time to close. A rip-roaring success, claimed Dooley as he clapped his customers on the shoulder and helped them into their overcoats.

"Come again boys another year! God bless you! And you, my darling. Sure you've got the loveliest voice of them all. Happy Christmas now. You've done a great thing today for the Lifeboats!"

His big frame filled the doorway as he waved them off and then we heard his feet on the stairs, returning to the chosen who stayed behind.

"That was bloody good, if I say so myself." He pulled the heavy curtains to, shut London out, set a new bottle of whiskey on the table and applied himself to the task of shuffling the cards. "I'll tell you what, lads. We'll top it all off by adding tonight's winnings to the collection. That's fair isn't it? That wipes out the sin of gambling over Christmas!" He cast a conspirator's glance at Mary, Joseph and the Shepherds and began to deal.

Nobody argued. We were all too sozzled to argue and as the stakes were particularly high that night, the Lifeboats did well and we rolled home thinking ourselves great philanthropists.

That was the start of a tradition that burgeoned year on year. Christmas Carol night would be sold out in June. The Covent Garden crowd returned with their friends and, to Dooley's delight, put on 'spontaneous' performances. So those who could not afford to dine in the bar would walk out of their way to hear the concert and the legendary finale that was Dooley's moment of glory. This year, after some teasing and cajoling, he took the part he had dreamed of singing in Rome - Allegri's 'Miserere' - and his top notes, belted out at a dozen decibels, brought all traffic to a standstill. We guffawed till our sides ached and the tears coursed down our cheeks and the cash kept rolling steadily in and little Donald sat blear-eyed in his corner, with a tombstone of Christmas Pudding on his plate. Everything went like clockwork till Mulligan stepped out of line.

Brendan Mulligan had joined our circle recently. A fellow-Irishman, he had slipped casually into Dooley's confidence and his insinuation amongst us had put several noses out of joint. Woodcock reckoned he was a cheat, but couldn't catch him at it.

For my part, I was simply jealous - I was one of Dooley's oldest chums, after all - so I felt a glow of satisfaction when the poodle got his come-uppance.

"Why must it always be the Lifeboats, you give to, Dooley? Sure, it's boring to do the same thing every year. You should swap around a bit. There's plenty more popular charities, and they'd get the celebrities in. You could double your impact, you know." He was dandling a twiglet in his beer and so did not see the look of wrath that Dooley turned his way.

"I'll make my own decisions thank-you," he snapped.

The other, intent upon his diversion, went on:

"I mean, what about that children's hospital? That would be a good one, now..."

Dooley had him suddenly on his feet, one giant hand gripping his collar, the other curled in a fist beneath his nose.

"I said *I'll make the decisions*! You want to run things - you go and do your *own* show - somewhere else. You got that?"

"Hey, Dooley, Dooley man!" whimpered the little fellow. "What's the matter? I don't mean any offence. You know me! I'm just blabbing with my big, Irish tongue. It's the whiskey talking! I don't mean to tread on your corns."

Dooley dropped him. "Well that's just what you have done. Right? It *has* to be the Lifeboats. Understand? *All* of you! I don't sing rotten carols for the love of it!"

He slumped down at the table and poured himself a drink. An uneasy silence descended while we cringed at the rebuke, like puppies that had never been kicked before. And in truth, was that not all we really were, dogs beneath the great man's table? Dooley played with us, humoured us, but we knew that his affairs had a wider sphere and that our stakes at poker were but a shadow of the real gambling he undertook elsewhere. He was horse-trading now with people so powerful they were invisible and their chips were the lumps of glass and steel rising from the Thames-side mud. Dangerous games. Small wonder if the man felt edgy.

Finally Wallace found his tongue: "My sister's gone to Capri. Well, *trying* to go. They've got as far as the airport and the stewards are all on strike."

144

"Happens every Christmas!" Newman leapt in.

We all tumbled after in a fugue of anecdotes, desperate to avoid another pause, but Dooley swung himself round and banged his bottle on the table.

"Enough of that! I'm sorry. Okay? Let's drink up now and be merry. No good sulking at Christmas!"

Somehow, it didn't quite work. We were too anxious to please, Dooley too hasty to forget. The kitchen staff crept in at the door. "All right to go now, Mr. Dooley? We're all done for the night."

"Go boys! Thanks for all your work. See you tomorrow. Hey, Seamus, that's a wonderful baritone you've been hiding all these months. How d'you get that? I'm thinking *you* should be at the opera."

The sous-chef snorted and ducked his head, embarrassed.

"Yelling in the kitchen!" replied his peers. "Oh, and at football matches!"

Dooley smiled. "Well it's great. You've all done just great. £2000 tonight. Annabel counted. Put off the lights in the passage as you go."

The chefs shuffled out and we began to deal.

In the darkened hush that followed, we played four games. Dooley was drinking all the time, not in a casual way, but steadily hoofing down great gulps. His face had taken on an ashen hue, his fingers lightly drummed on the table. At any moment, we expected him to leap again to his feet. But he had gained command of himself and when he next spoke it was with a compelling composure.

"If you really want to know, I'll tell you."

Effortlessly, we tacked this sentence, as intended, onto Mulligan's earlier exchange. We forgot the assault as though it had never happened. Now we sat forward, tense and expectant, our faces, sculpted by the candle-light into crude Goyescas: holes for eye-sockets, smears and gashes for lips.

"It happened nine years ago, in Wales," said Dooley. "At Christmas time.

"It was just at the start of my property career. You could still pick up the occasional gem for a bargain price, if you were prepared to put in the necessary restoration work and I began to invest in a string of holiday places in Wales. Sea views - saints and history - all that stuff. Never failed to pull the punters in. I had four or five up and running and an office overlooking Tenby harbour, with a very pretty receptionist. Thought I was quite the lad, I did. I'd work from home in Esher and pop up every now and then, if a new opening came along. Well, I had other irons in the fire, as you can imagine, but this receptionist - let's say she was an incentive to keep the Pembrokeshire project going.

"Alice, she was. Long dark hair. Rosebud mouth. A tan in the middle of winter. Sure, I wasn't blind and I knew she liked me. So when the church at Llangwaer came onto the market, I packed my bags right away. This could turn out to be a developer's dream: ancient stones and state of the art technology. A whirlpool bath, dishwasher, microwave, and that new miracle, wireless internet.

"The site at Llangwaer lay so steeped in legend, I could hardly believe my ears. A sixth century chapel on the cliff-top, with a holy well beside it. An Ogham-carved stone, dating back to the time of the Romans. Steps down the cliff to a beach where the seals were singing... What more need I say! The place had fallen into disuse twenty years before and had become a squat for a hippy called Harry who lived there, making eco-sculptures until he thankfully passed away. But the deal would be complicated.

"Welsh Tourism, in conjunction with the Church of England and the regional Heritage Board wanted Llangwaer as part of their Pilgrims and Saints Experience: a cultural theme tour taking visitors to sites of interest. They had all the authorities on their side - only they didn't have the money! *I* had cash on the nail - but everyone from the parish council to the landlord of the nearest pub was against me. Some local johnny, who wrote romantic novels, mounted a 'Save Llangwaer' campaign and collected a thousand signatures but what they didn't, or couldn't know, was that there was nothing I loved more than a battle. I was going to relish every bloody minute."

Dooley stretched his legs. Now that he had got into his story, some of the strain had gone out of his face. Like a man in a confessional, parcelling up his tale and pushing it through the grill, he seemed to feel his burden lighten. He would not stop now till the whole thing was out.

"First time I visited was in the summer. You needed a four-by-four to get down the track. You could see the little, grey bell-tower cutting the long cliff-line, three hundred yards away. There was a froth of hogweed, four or five foot high, swamping the tombstones but in my mind's eye, I could already picture it as it would look in the brochure: emerald lawns, patio table and chairs - a discreet hot-tub, perhaps, with a view of the sea...

"We had had a drought all summer and the little well nearby had gone down to a trickle - then dried up - first time in thirty years. The stone shelter that housed it stood apart from the church in a patch of field, but the thing was derelict. I'd call it sacrilege. I'm as lapsed as they come, but even *I* was shocked.

That so-called eco-artist had decked the place with fetishistic trash - recycling, I suppose he called it. Old Dinky toys, doll's heads, petrol cans, magazine cuttings, cigarette packets - they were all over the grotto, together with his precious thoughts, all scribbled in graffiti; an altar to world peace; his teapot and the ashes of the fire he brewed his kettle on. Visitors had chucked in charms and pennies and tied bits of filthy rag on the hawthorn trees. *Greens!* What's the point of them, I'd like to know?

"Anyhow, we pressed on to the church. Even in ruins it had an undeniable charm. The rain from Ireland drives clean onto this coast and every stone of the churchyard wall had sprouted ferns and mosses - green and fresh and never mind the drought. It made me think of my old home, it did. I opened the gate with a sense of destiny. This place was going to be mine and no one would stand in my way. In the same spirit I chucked away a withered Christmas wreath that crowned the gatepost. More trash, I thought. Not on my site. Not now!

"I've got photos, still, of how it was - the toppling graves, the broken slates, the massive, rusted padlock on the door, that would not yield to the key I had been given. Brambles and creepers had

147

reclaimed the building. You could see them, nodding at the windows from the *in*side, where they had thrust up through the chancel slabs. Panes were broken here and there but the sun streamed in on the western side and, by standing on a drain, I could make out what was left of the interior: a solitary pulpit - a bench or two. Ropes and buckets lay as if work had been suspended without warning. My hippy, being unable to pick the lock, must have confined his activities to the well and the 'garden' which he had created round his van; the centrepiece of this feature, - an upturned boat with a pink, neoprene angel sitting astride it.

"'We get this lot out straightaway!' I said to my manager. "I want space here..." and in a sudden moment of inspiration. "I tell you what we'll do. We'll split the site! Look, I can't have people cooking their kebabs with a lot of graves all round them. The barbeque goes here. We'll move the headstones over there by the well. Patio here. Hedge here. There's no reason why the council can't *keep* the well and still do their Heritage tours. I might even let them have the Ogham stone. And *I'll* have the church and I'll turn it into the finest property in Wales! That way they get their money - and I get my business. There's just the matter of this odd grave here. It doesn't fit the theme. Too new. 1974. That was the year the church was decommissioned. Only a young woman, too. Find out who she was - if she's got relatives living. We might have to quietly lose this one."

"Well, my diplomacy won the day. They don't call me Dexterous Dooley for nothing! I returned to Esher and my Welsh team set to work, transforming the place according to plan. Piles of architect's drawings, bathroom designs, door-handle samples, cess-pit brochures, all the finer details, landed for approval on my desk. By an ironic twist of Fate, we had to go 'green'. It was simply too costly to run mains connections there so we opted for solar power and a system which extracted heat from the ground! But by then I was able to see the funny side. I'd made my peace with that old hippy Harry. Construction work was finished in October. That gave us three months to advertise before the new season kicked off and the contractors promised total completion by Christmas. The only loser was the novelist, though I reckon he got another book, at least, out of his campaign!

"That Christmas I had a few things to celebrate and it occurred to me that I owed myself a treat. I had been working day and night - if you can call driving bargains *working* - and hadn't had a break for months. I reckoned I deserved a holiday. Why shouldn't *I* have first pick of staying at Llangwaer, and take the lovely Alice along with me? She was keen enough. She had a Granny in Haverfordwest. She would visit her and then drive on down to the coast on Christmas Eve, while I got the log burner going and set the champagne on ice. We'd give the place a proper christening. I had designed it, after all, with seduction in mind. Deep pile carpets, soft, leather sofas, a circular bed upstairs - everything white! There were white, fluffy bath robes, with throw-away slippers and fat, white candles and cushions - a dining table à-deux, tucked into a mirrored recess - flat-screen t.v. There is something so addictive about surrounding oneself with new things. I love them. I love ripping off the cellophane and savouring the acrylic smell. I suppose I thought it would be the same with Alice. I had something of a reputation, as you know, in that department!"

Dooley almost allowed himself a smile, but then he returned to his monologue and his face was grave once more.

"Anyhow, it wasn't to be. That Christmas Eve it started to snow. I didn't think anything of it. In my Class A four-wheel-drive, I ploughed on towards the iron horizon, intent upon my prize. Alice had a good car - I had made sure of that - and she could phone at any time if she was in trouble. It was best if I went on ahead; opened the gates and put the heating on. We had tarmacked the rutted pilgrim's track that led down to Llangwaer, even put in lay-bys for tourist coaches, but by the time I reached Fishguard, I was glad that my tyres were like corrugated drums. The snow was settling fast as the light was fading and it would be all I could do to reach the church before dusk.

"There were fairy lights in the fish and chip shop by the harbour and a lone Christmas tree at the petrol station, but the town itself felt bleak: a maze of empty holiday houses, and boarded-up shop windows. Since the coming of the Quids-In Superstore, the only businesses *in business* seemed to be hairdressers and their clients had taken a final look in the mirror, paid their tips and taken their Christmas faces home.

"As I climbed the hill, I began to have misgivings. Suppose the Thomases had not ordered the logs and aired the beds as arranged? Suppose my key didn't fit? I had relished the weight of it - the great lump of iron we had had forged for the lock - as I slipped it into my pocket that morning. Driving in shirt sleeves (the dashboard thermostat read twenty-four) I fumbled for the jacket, hanging behind me. The key was safe there, still.

"Now came high hedges, the rooftops of the village bungalows. *Take this right fork.* Snow flared and spun in my headlights. Here was the coast road and the half-buried sign: 'Llangwaer Holy Well ½ mile'. So far my new sat-nav had done me proud. Now I could turn off the radio and let the silence seep in. That would be the lay-by for coaches - tourist sign there - here the entrance to the drive. The automatic gates shuddered back, heaping snow on either side and I glided through and - Oh my God! - I almost stalled on the spot. That sight will never leave me! The Thomases had been, and left lights on in welcome. I can't tell you the sense of pride I felt when I saw the beauty of the place - the lamplight on the snow - how immaculate it was! - and a Christmas tree winking from the sanctuary window.

"I had no need to worry about the key fitting, either. It slipped into the lock like magic and the door swung back without a sound. Holy Mary! I can tell you, I felt like a bridegroom seeing his wedding night bride! Of course, I had had photos - dozens of them - but to be *standing* on the threshold, with the white carpet lapping at my feet, the smell of the Christmas spices air-freshener already in my nose - well, for a moment I quite forgot about Alice. This was *my* creation. From the mouldy, worm-eaten, bramble-ridden ruin I had first discovered, I had created this gleaming haven; a monument to entrepreneurial skill and grit. And if that wasn't something to be proud of, then I didn't care what was! I brought in the bags, and the champagne and the 21 carat gold watch I had bought to go with it. And then I got Alice's text.

"'Hi mark, sorry can't make it tonight. Snow too heavy in h'west. gran had a fall so im staying with her. Tried to phone but signal here terrible. Happy xmas. Love you. A xxx'

"Rage is no cure for impotence, but in my disappointment I felt so badly used, I railed against the snow, the satellites, the weakness of women; everything which had conspired to lure me into this trap. Was it the Grandmother who had warned her off? Then the fall just about served her right! Was Alice truly sorry? Then I was glad she wouldn't be having the watch! Now I found myself stranded, completely alone, on a headland about as far from civilization as it is possible to be, and I would be there, marooned, possibly for days, with nothing on earth to do. Promising myself a rest, I had not even brought my computer.

"Instantly, the charm of the festive lights fell flat, and pleasure shrivelled. Such is the power of the mind, I no longer had an appetite for turkey or brie-and-cranberry canapés. The very thought of mince pies, even the tipsy, star-topped ones from Fortnum's, made my guts heave. And I was getting cold on the doorstep and had no option but to unload my luggage and make the best of things, for it would be no use now seeking a hotel elsewhere. I'd as likely end up in a snow-drift and spend the night in the car.

"Llangwaer church door, with its well-oiled latch, shut like the lid of a coffin on my Christmas hopes.

"As you might expect, the phone was dead. And though my underground energy system went on pumping out buckets of power - in fact the place blazed like a lighthouse - neither radio, nor television could restore to me the sense that I was part of the living world. Indeed, festive hilarity seemed so out of place to my jaundiced mood, I turned both off and resorted instead to silence.

"Silence! Have you ever heard the authentic thing? It comes down like a smothering fog. It fills your ears till you think that they will burst. It is a terrible, pitiless, utterly implacable thing. At first I busied myself about - took a shower, found my slippers, poured a tumbler of Scotch. Every sound of life dropped into that silence and drowned, like the wick of a paraffin lamp which has sunk too low. I can hear, to this day, the chink of my glass on the hearthstone, the patter of snow at the window-panes as the wind wrapped itself around the walls; the beat of my own heart - eyes dilated, pulse thumping, as I stared at the patch of the carpet at my feet. I tried coughing, clearing my throat, muttering things - God help me, I even attempted to sing. The silence crept back, soaking up all trace of what had been. And then I began to give way to foolish thoughts.

"In my mind's eye, I pictured the well, and the tombstones that had once been tumbled about, like rotten teeth, not twenty yards away. I knew that they had been arranged, all nice and tidy, in their new plot - but I hadn't actually *been*. Now I seemed to see a grim procession of the old ones trudging back across the snow, to find their rightful beds. I had a horrible presentiment that the ghost of Hairy Harry was out there too, boiling his herbal tea, surrounded by all his ghoulish paraphernalia... Perhaps... Oh God! And then I heard it! Unmistakable. A sound that cut through the air, but lingered on - the cry of a woman, somewhere, calling for help. I tell you the blood froze in my veins. I thought of all the horror films I had seen - werewolves, vampires, mummies - everything I had ever laughed at, crowded in, and in my panic I began to pray. After all, this was once a place of sanctuary, and you know, once a Catholic... you never forget the words: '*Hail Mary, full of grace...*' I didn't get very far.

"Knifing through the night came that cry again, somewhere to the south, where the path led through the fields towards the cliff. Anguished and desperate, I heard it now as a human voice. Somebody was in trouble.

"With a monumental effort I pulled myself together, grabbed a torch from the cupboard under the stairs, threw on my overcoat and stepped outside. The snow had settled and drifted. It came up over my shoes, almost a foot thick in places and whirled around me in a blinding mass, but by the lights of the building I picked out my car and the gate, and the distant hump of the well. I wouldn't be able to get very far, but I could call and at least I had reassured myself that there were no old Welshmen wandering round the garden. My voice carried out across the waste: "Where are you? Hallooo!"

"Nothing came back. I walked as far as the lay-by - circled the well, the burial plot, turned around and headed the other way, towards the coast. There were no footprints there. I didn't dare step off the road, but I called and called again. No reply came back. If she had fainted, whoever she was, she wouldn't last long in this, but I had no way of raising an alarm, and by now I was beginning to wonder if I had imagined it all.

"Irishmen are given to fancying things, but I must say I had now got a grip on the facts and I reasoned it out like this. If I went on roaming about in that snowstorm I would soon be dead myself. My thin, cashmere coat was no use against such weather. I would go back to the porch and listen again. If I heard so much as whimper, I would head back for the village and mount a proper rescue. If not, I would down another drink and try to survive the night as best I could. First thing tomorrow, by whatever possible means, I was heading back for civilization!

"Well, I waited till my bones were chilled and at last, with some reluctance, went indoors. There, by the fire, sat a young woman, half-naked, shivering and soaked to the skin. She had left a trail of wet footprints behind her and, to this day, I don't know whether I was relieved or appalled to see her.

"'What, in the name of ...

"She put up a hand to stop me.

"'I had an accident down by the shore,' she said. 'I put out a call for help, but in this weather the coastguards can't get through.'

"'Holy Mother of God, what happened?'

"She closed her eyes, put her hand to her mouth as if trying to find an answer, then gave it up and waved the intention away. She looked vulnerable, weak - too weak to cry...

"'No matter!' I leapt into action. 'You'll be all right now, darling. Don't you worry. I heard you shouting. It *was* you shouting, wasn't it? I went out there to find you. Put your wet things off, before you freeze to death. I'll fetch a blanket. God, you look a mess! Not hurt, I hope?"

"She shook her head.

"'Well, that's a mercy.' Silently, I began to assess the damage she had done. My lovely carpet! Mud, sand, seaweed and dirty snow were scattered in clots across the virgin pile. *Some christening*! I thought regretfully. *Some almighty bill to pay, and before the place had ever even been used*! But at least I had proof of a palpable body before me - I was not hallucinating or imagining or going round the twist. And that was something.

"When I returned, I found her, unabashed, removing the last of her clothes.

"'Here put this round you. And pull your chair up to the fire. A sip of this won't hurt you, either. When you feel better, you can tell me your name.'

"'Mary Ann,' says she, cool as the proverbial cucumber.

"'Have you stopped shaking yet?' Water was seeping out of her hair and glistening on the blanket. Her hands were streaked with grime, nails clogged with it. I couldn't help staring as she cradled her drink in her lap and the firelight played on her face. After the initial shock, I didn't know what to think. I felt waves of conflicting emotions: revulsion, fascination, a kind of curious excitement...

"'Are there others?' I asked. 'People waiting for you?' And for the first time she looked me straight in the eye.

"'Oh, no.' Her hand strayed to cover her knee. 'I'm all alone. No need to worry.'

"'I'll run you a bath!' I said. Better to break the tension now. 'It's a Jacuzzi, too. That'll warm you up a treat! Then we'll find some food. Bathroom's this way. Soap and everything - it's all right there. Just help yourself."

"'I'm glad I saw your light,' she said. 'God knows how I would have managed otherwise.'

"'Don't even think about it now.' Already, I was planning ahead. The microwave-ready Beef Bourguignon, Château Lafite '72, Crème Brûlée pots and Columbian coffee might just come in handy after all.

"But when she emerged from the vestry, new-bathed, in her fluffy, white robe, golden hair gleaming, eyes shining, I have to confess that I lost my interest in food. Her shredded denims cast aside, she assumed a beauty that put young Alice in the shade. Here was a real woman who needed comfort. And boys, you know me, I'm *all* heart. If there was any man at that time, adept in the business of comforting women, I was that man, and I can tell you it was a relief to me to find that she had no fancy qualms or coy pretences about accepting what was on offer.

"Without the need for chatter or pointless preliminaries, we made straight for the softness of the circular bed and the pleasures of mutual discovery..."

Dooley broke off and placed his finger-tips together, pressing his hands against his lips like a priest about to say grace, while we - we sat in expectant silence; our lewd minds, sprawled supine.

"'Oh, lads.' He groaned at last. 'I don't know how to begin to tell you... How to go on at all... Mary Ann was like no ordinary woman. She felt cold, ice cold still, and with her firm flesh and slippery, silky skin she had a feel like no human *I'd* ever touched. I tell you, it was like lying beside a giant, fresh-caught mackerel. But that was not the worst of it... Neither that, nor the salty, fishy smell that clung about her... I may have drawn back at that point, but she, she was not so shy. She put her arms about me and smothered me in an embrace that was like the grip of death itself. How long she held me I cannot say. Her lips congealed to mine; her cold heart throbbed at my chest. She sucked all the vitality out of me. Gasping, I felt the chill of her invade my bones, but struggle was futile and in the end I believe my breath expired. My very soul departed from my body and drifted free, unhoused, in the midnight air. I sank into oblivion and I did not wake till the bell in the bell tower roused me, ringing the faithful to prayer on Christmas morning. God's truth, I heard it! You can call me absurd, hysterical, or just plain drunk, but I swear that *that* and that alone summoned my scattered wits and opened my eyes to the blessed light of day.

"The alarm clock by my bed said ten o'clock. I started up like a maniac, thinking I would be late for choir, all my bearings lost. But of course, there was no church - no faithful - no service. No Mary Ann either. The rumpled sheets lay round me in a foaming mass, but Mary Ann had vanished as mysteriously as she had come, taking her muddy footprints with her. Neither in the bathroom, nor in the kitchen, was there any sign that another had been in the house. And fresh snow had erased all evidence of coming and going outside. My empty whisky bottle, which lay discarded in the hearth, gave its own account of what had happened and filled my mind with shame. Dooley! Dooley getting old and unable to handle his drink! But no matter how hard I tried to reason this way, I still could not shake off a sense of the blank, the awful horror which had nearly claimed me.

"I packed my bags, turned out the lights and locked the door forever on Llangwaer Retreat. With a demon energy I dug my car out of the drifts, like a taphephobe digging his way out of the grave; battled up the deserted lane, back to the bungalows in the village - the turning for PenParrog - the main road... Oh, God be thanked! There was the petrol station - the Angel Inn, with a man, real flesh and blood, sweeping the steps! Nothing could hold me now. I was done with Wales. I was coming back to the living world and I'd never put foot in that hell-hole again.

"Once back in Esher, I set about packing up my Pembrokeshire assets - sold them, lock stock and barrel, (Alice included), to another developer. And I turned my sights on other prospects.

"I tried to forget that Christmas and everything associated with it; buried it out of sight. From that day to this, I have never told a living soul what I have just told you and I have never touched another woman, either. Gambling and drink are vices enough to keep a man going steady, eh?

He tried to laugh, but we sensed that there was more to come, and sure enough, his face grew solemn and he resumed his tale:

"Everything went well for a little while. I pulled off some lucky deals, bought this place, became a name to be reckoned with. Then one day, about four years ago, *he* arrived...

He jerked his head towards the corner where Donald lay slumped. We felt a sudden unease - the shadow of guilt and shame, I suppose, which that poor figure of neglect always threw over us - and edged a little closer on our seats. Oblivious to us, Dooley continued, without breaking his sentence:

"...in a taxi, with a bag of clothes and a bunch of official papers. Four years old. No return address." Another pause. "It wouldn't normally have been a problem. I mean, I had fought off paternity suits before. Well, as you know, I *did* have a bit of a reputation, there. But this was different. This..." he fumbled for a word,

"...*creature* - came with no past, no memory, no spark of communication. Just an envelope with the child allowance forms, letters from social services - everything all in order, mind - and a birth certificate: *Date of birth September 25th 2005. Pembroke Royal Hospital. Father: Mark Alistair Dooley. Mother: Mary Ann Caisters.*'"

"My first thought was to go straight to the police, but then, wary of the publicity, I thought I'd do my own researches first. My cleaning woman, Betty, would look after the boy, meanwhile. First check that no child of this description had been reported missing. Then find the mother. That name, Mary Ann, filled me with a sense of dread. Social Services proved no help at all. Most attentive, they were; confirmed that all was legal and correct - checks and interviews all properly recorded. They would call very soon to offer support and advice. They were not at liberty to disclose the mother's whereabouts. Pembroke hospital proved equally opaque.

"But my man, a hired detective - well, I had no choice, lads, had I? - had better luck at the Tenby Records Office. And his news made no sense to any but me. A Mary Ann Caisters appeared on file, with birth and death certificates, census records, and a rather lengthy coroner's report. Born in Berkshire, a writer of travel guides, she had drowned when her boat capsized off the Pembrokeshire coast, Christmas 1974. She was buried, by public subscription, in a place called Llangwaer, close to the scene of the wreck. Upon my orders Giles made further enquiries. Locals at Penparrog had little to say about Mary Ann. She was the last person to be buried at the church before it was decomissioned and her grave stone had been turned out with the others when the ancient tombs were moved. She had neither relatives nor friends to object when the committee decided her stone, being modern, looked out of keeping in the well-side plot, and quietly lost it under the toilet block. She had been alone at the time of the accident - a difficult, headstrong woman. She had set out to sea against good advice. The Coastguards hadn't a hope of finding her - not in weather like that. Such folk put other's lives at risk. There was scant sympathy for her at the Angel Inn.

157

"Now what, tell me truly, what was I to think? That somebody, Alice say, had pulled this scam on me out of revenge? But I had never had the pleasure of 'knowing' Alice and who would go to such lengths to palm off an innocent boy on a stranger? Besides, as I told you, no word of the Llangwaer affair had ever passed my lips.

"Look at him. Looks an angel, doesn't he? But he's not like other boys. I don't honestly know what he is! He fills me with horror every time I clap eyes on him! He is my conscience - my mortality - my damnation! And we are bound together as if we were already in purgatory - the criminal and his crime, forced to dance together. And the only angel *I* can see when I look at him is the pink plastic one astride the keel of that boat at Llangwaer. That was *her*, wasn't it? And to think - to think she must have visited Hairy Harry too, or why would he have made the thing at all? Oh, it's too obscene to think about!

The lads had shuffled to their feet, embarrassed to see Dooley abase himself in this way. One by one, they mumbled their excuses, and, like all the world's gambling friends when misfortune strikes, melted into the night. All but me. Why it was I cannot tell. Perhaps the sight of that god-forsaken boy called up memories of my own troubled past, and moved me to stay behind. For the first time in my adult life, I felt the stirrings of a feeling that turned my heart upside down. Looking back, I suppose it was pity. For Dooley, for Donald, for myself. At the door I turned and surprised myself by speaking out:

"Dooley, does it really matter?" I saw him suddenly stripped of his glamour, an ageing inebriate, a man who could not trust his friends or even his memory to hold true. "Does it matter *what* the boy is? He's just a boy. Maybe he's yours or maybe someone else's. Maybe his mother *was* a mermaid. Maybe you had too much whisky! He's still a boy. Surely you'd do more to save your soul by loving him and making him your own, than by gambling for the Lifeboats, no? It's too late for the Lifeboats. They can't save Mary Ann now. But you could get them to replace her tombstone - even send a wreath at Christmas..."

Dooley gave me such a look I thought for a moment he was going to knock me down. He stood like a man transfixed. Then, gradually, the fear receded from his eyes and at length he stirred, recovered his composure and pushed his hand through his hair.

"Perhaps I shall have to start believing in miracles, after all," he said. "Sure to God, Simon, that's the first sensible thing I've heard you say in all me life! You mean, *make* the boy my son! It would mean the end of gambling; the end of Dooley's speculation empire; the cut-throats, liars and good-for-nothings, like *you*. There would be no time for any of that. And the Bar, what would become of the Bar?" He was planning already, with the quicksilver acuity that had made him great. He cast another glance at the sleeping child and when his eyes next met mine they shone with glee:

"Could be the greatest gamble of them all, don't you think? *That boy* against the whole of the rest of the world? Sure, Simon, You're a genius, after all!"

"Good night, Dooley," I said, suddenly choked with emotion. "Happy Christmas."

I cast a last glance at the wooden crib, the guttering candles and the lad who had cast me out. "God bless you," I murmured from the depths of my astonished heart. "God bless you and every child like you!"

Also by Rosemary Pavey

Two novels, exploring the landscape of childhood - enthralling for the imaginative reader

Suitable for 12 years+

Amazon Reviews:

"...up there with the classics of the genre for suspense, style and fun."

"...seasoned readers will find great depths of thought and learning woven into the plot."

"...think the Hobbit versus Dr. No."

"...a very satisfying read."

These books are available online from Amazon or can be purchased direct through www.paveypenandpaint.com

The Magpie's Nest

A Summer School

The first of the Trudi Larsson stories...

The Larssons are a model, modern family: successful parents, clever children, a comfortable, suburban home. Everything seems just fine until Grandfather Larsson comes to stay. Then uneasy cracks appear. Old Per brings draughts of a subversive other-world from his forest-home in Sweden and within days of his arrival the household's careful summer plans are in disarray.

While her parents fume at the disruption, ten-year-old Trudi is intrigued by Per. Why is he so secretive about his past? And where does he go when he should be asleep in his bed? And how does he contrive to know things no one has ever told him? In defiance of everyone, she sets her heart on uncovering the truth.

Gradually her safe, suburban world reveals hidden depths. Trudi finds herself on a path which will bring her face to face with her darkest fears, but by now there can be no turning back... She has already been bewitched, for Grandfather Larsson is no ordinary grandfather and his secrets are the secrets of enchantment.

Did you think that magic was child's play? Think again.

'A journey to the interior of things is an adventure for any curious mind and everything is curious for those with eyes to see.

The Beehive Cluster

A Novel for All Ages

Trudi Larsson's second adventure...

On a fragile planet with few choices left, technology promises magic solutions, but if reality can be re-mastered at the touch of a button, how can one know what is actually true? And what place is left for the old magic of the imagination?

These are questions at the heart of Rosemary Pavey's tale. For the young rebel, Trudi, they become a battleground between the mythic world of her half-Sami grandfather and the machinations of a plot to steal the blueprint of life.

Bees, stars and spindle whorls... From Inca legend to Arctic snow, the story takes a roller-coaster ride, charting landscapes invisible to the ordinary eye.

Here you will find humour, adventure, skulduggery and the breathtaking patterns of the cosmos.

Welcome to the world of The Beehive Cluster...

Hold tight, for things are not quite what they seem!

Rosemary Pavey has worked as a freelance artist in Sussex for over 25 years.

Visit www.paveypenandpaint.com to view the full range of paintings, drawings, prints and cards available at her Ditchling Studio.